Sadie Rose

AND THE COTTONWOOD CREEK ORPHAN

The Lord's Prayer

Our Father in heaven, hallowed be Your name. Your kingdom come. Your will be done on earth as it is in heaven. Give us this day our daily bread. And forgive us our debts, as we forgive our debtors. And do not lead us into temptation, but deliver us from the evil one. For Yours is the kingdom and the power and the glory forever. Amen.

This Book Belongs to

Courtney Mengel

A PRAIRIE FAMILY ADVENTURE

Sadie Rose
AND THE
COTTONWOOD
CREEK ORPHAN

Hilda Stahl

CROSSWAY BOOKS • WESTCHESTER, ILLINOIS 60153
A DIVISION OF GOOD NEWS PUBLISHERS

Dedicated with love to
Carol Farley

Cover illustration by Kathy Kulin

Overall book design by Karen L. Mulder

Third printing, 1990

Printed in the United States of America

Library of Congress Catalog Card Number 88-71808

ISBN 0-89107-513-5

Contents

1

The Search

Sadie flung the dishwater over the sandy ground beside the soddy where Momma had planted flowers last week. Sadie knew not to waste water, even water that she'd washed breakfast dishes in for the whole family. Her braids flipped on her thin shoulders. The hot Nebraska wind whipped flecks of water back against her worn dress and bare feet. From inside the soddy she heard Opal laugh at something Momma had said.

Just then Helen peeked around the corner of the sod house. Her small face was almost as white as her baby-fine hair, and her blue eyes were wide with worry. "Sadie," Helen whispered. "Sadie!"

Sadie glanced back inside the soddy where Momma and Opal were filling pillow ticks with clean, soft duck feathers, then ran to Helen. "What's wrong?" Sadie kept her voice down too.

"Bossie's gone." Helen looked quickly around to make sure no one was near, then gripped Sadie's hand. "I really and truly did make sure she was staked out and couldn't get away, but she pulled loose and she's gone. So's Babe."

Sadie sucked in her breath. "Did you tell Web?"

Helen looked horrified. She was eight and he was nine, and they were both supposed to watch Bossie and her new calf so the coyotes wouldn't get the calf. "No! He'd tell Momma. I thought you and me could go look for them and get them back before anyone noticed."

Sadie frowned out across the wide treeless prairie. Wind rippled the grass. White fluffy clouds dotted the blue sky. Neither Bossie nor her calf were in sight. "I'll get the rifle." Last month when they'd moved from Douglas County in eastern Nebraska across the state to the rim of the sandhills to live with York on his homestead he'd told them if they ever went far away from the house they were to take a gun with them. "You never know when a rattlesnake might want to say howdy," York had said with his slow Texas drawl and his ready laugh.

Helen twisted her thin, dirt-covered hands into her faded apron. "Please hurry, Sadie. Bossie's been gone a long time already. I don't want a coyote to eat Babe."

Sadie sucked in her breath again and forced back the sharp scolding words on the tip of her tongue. Momma had said many times that even though Sadie was twelve, she couldn't boss Helen or Web around. Opal and Riley often bossed them all. Riley at sixteen thought he was a man already, especially since Pa had died and Momma had married York. York had given Riley a wide-brimmed hat and boots to make him look like a rancher instead of a farmer. Riley would walk over cactus barefoot if York asked him to because Riley had always wanted to be a cowboy. At fourteen Opal was waiting to be sixteen so she could find a nice young man and get married and have babies of her own.

Her hand steady, but her stomach fluttering, Sadie hung the dishpan in place beside the washstand and lifted the rifle from over the door. "Momma, I'll shoot dinner." It wasn't a lie. She'd hunt for grouse or prairie chicken or rabbit while they hunted for Bossie and Babe. "Helen's goin' with me."

Momma nodded without looking up from the pillow. "Wear your bonnet. And don't waste bullets."

"I won't, Momma." Sadie dropped the box of shells in her apron pocket, then tied her faded bonnet at her chin.

Opal shot Sadie a look as if she knew something was going on, but she didn't say anything.

The rifle at her side, Sadie strode past the well and out into the vast prairie with Helen beside her. "Put on your bonnet, Helen."

Helen lifted her bonnet off her back and tied it in place. Sadie and Helen had made the bonnet themselves out of one of Helen's worn-out dresses. Once the dress had been a lovely pink with tiny pink and yellow and blue flowers all over it. Now it was almost gray with just a hint that flowers had ever covered it. The tiny pieces that had been left over from the bonnet had gone into Web's quilt.

"I don't know how Bossie got loose," said Helen.

"She hates being staked out," Sadie answered.

Birds flew through the wide blue sky and perched on the swaying grasses and sang into the constant Nebraska wind. In the distance Sadie heard the squawk of York's windmill, hidden from sight by the rolling hills.

Beside her she heard Helen praying under her breath.

Sadie bit her lip. Just this morning York had said that God was her loving Heavenly Father, that He was always with her. Sometimes she wondered if that was true. She'd thought Pa would always be with her, but he'd died in a blizzard. He'd gone to get her so she wouldn't get lost in the blizzard and he'd gotten lost himself. They'd buried his body near their homestead in Douglas County, but he'd gone to live in Heaven with Jesus. Pa hadn't been with her always like she'd always thought he'd be. Maybe God was like Pa. She knew God could never die, but maybe He'd go away from her. The thought brought a tear to Sadie's eye, and she blinked it quickly away.

Helen stopped at the top of a small hill and looked around, slowly turning. An ant crawled across her bare foot, and she shook it off. "I don't see 'em."

Sadie shifted the weight of the rifle and sighed. They had to find Bossie and Babe. York had about three hundred head of cattle, but they were for beef, not milking. Bossie had walked all the way from Douglas County with them tied behind the covered wagon because Momma had insisted on keeping her milk cow. Momma didn't want to go without milk and butter and cottage cheese.

A coyote ran across the flat land between two hills, its long flag of a tail waving behind it. Sadie's hand tightened on the rifle. She wanted to shoot the coyote, but she knew she'd probably miss at that distance.

"Please, God, keep our calf safe from the coyotes," whispered Helen with a break in her voice. Suddenly she dashed down the hill, her arms waving like windmills to keep her balance.

Sadie cupped her free hand to her mouth. "Bossie!

Come, Boss! Come, Boss!" She choked. All her life she'd heard Pa call the cows that way. York never had. He was a cowboy, and he said he'd never milked a cow in his life except at the rodeo in the wild cow milking contest, but that didn't count.

"Come on, Sadie!" shouted Helen impatiently.

Sadie cradled the rifle in her arms and ran to Helen's side. They walked around a hill and Sadie stopped, listening intently. She started to take a step when she heard Bossie bawling as if she was in trouble. Helen heard her too and raced in the direction of the sound. Sadie followed, her braids bouncing on her shoulders. The grass felt warm against her bare feet.

At the base of the nearby small hill the wind had whipped away the side of it, leaving a big sandy blowout. Bossie, with Babe close to her side, her head down and her legs planted firmly, held a pack of snarling coyotes at bay. Sadie's heart jerked, and fear pricked her skin.

Helen clamped her hand over her mouth and stepped close to Sadie.

Two coyotes yapped and jumped forward, trying to scare Babe away from Bossie's protection. Bossie bellered, shaking her head, and the coyotes slinked back to join the others. Sadie counted seven coyotes. Two of them stood still, three of them paced back and forth yapping sharply, and the other two rested on their haunches, their tongues hanging out. Sadie raised her rifle and took aim, but she was too afraid Bossie or Babe would move and she'd hit them. She thought about shooting into the air, but she knew that would be a waste of a precious bullet.

"What're we going to do?" whispered Helen.

"Scare them away." Sadie sounded surer than she

felt. Sweat soaked her hands and made it hard to hold the rifle. She swallowed hard. "We'll have to get closer."

Helen gulped. "What if a coyote eats me?"

"York said they're afraid of humans." Sadie rubbed first one palm and then another down her apron. "Let's go. But we'll have to be careful not to scare Babe away from Bossie."

"Or the coyotes will eat her." Helen sounded close to tears.

"Let's go," Sadie said again. She walked so fast Helen had to run to keep up with her. "Come, Boss!" shouted Sadie.

Bossie turned her head and mooed loud and long. Babe jumped stiffly and bumped against her mother. The coyotes leaped away, but stopped and slunk toward Bossie and Babe again.

"Let's yell and run right toward the coyotes," said Sadie.

"Oh my," said Helen.

Sadie's heart raced, and fear made her shake. She looked down at Helen. "Ready?"

Helen nodded. "Wait!"

"What for?"

"What'll we yell, Sadie?"

"I don't know. It doesn't matter. Yell anything you want." Sadie took a deep breath. "Ready?"

Helen rubbed her hand over her thin chest. "Yes. But I don't know what to yell."

Sadie leaped forward with a cry that rang across the prairie. She saw the coyotes leap away, then hesitate as if they were wondering if they really had to leave behind a fine meal of freshly killed calf. "Run, you coyotes! Run! Leave our cow and calf alone, you coyotes!"

"You mean cousins to wolves!" cried Helen as she ran forward. She'd heard others call coyotes that, and she thought it sounded funny. "You mean cousins to wolves, you get away from our cow and our calf!" She glanced sideways at Sadie. "Am I doin' okay?"

"Yes."

"They're runnin'!" Helen jumped up and down, flapping her arms.

Sadie wanted to shoot the coyotes as they ran, but she knew she'd miss them. York and Riley could've brought the coyotes down with a single shot for each, but she wasn't that good. "Run, you coyotes! Run away and hide!" The words bounced out of her mouth as she raced after the fleeing coyotes. "Yip! Yip! Yip! You're nothin' but a bunch of scaredy-cats!"

"Scaredy-cat coyotes!" yelled Helen. She giggled. "Scaredy-cat coyotes."

Just then Sadie's foot caught on a creeping plant, and she crashed to the ground with a thud. Sand gritted in her teeth. Her breath whooshed out of her body, and the rifle flew from her hands. It landed several feet away on a barrel cactus.

Helen suddenly noticed she was running alone, and she stopped dead and looked back to see Sadie flat on her face. "Sadie!" Helen ran to her and dropped beside her. "What's wrong?"

Bossie mooed.

"Get the gun," gasped Sadie, trying to push herself up. She was too weak. "The gun, Helen."

Helen ran to the rifle and picked it up carefully, the way she'd been taught since she was old enough to carry it. Just then she heard a growl behind her, and she whirled around. A coyote crouched just a few feet from her, its fangs bared. She screamed so loud her throat hurt. Without thinking she leaped toward the coyote, using the gun like a club, swinging it at the coyote. "Get, you coyote! Get out of here now!"

Sadie jumped up, ignoring her pain, and ran at the coyote, yelling, "Get away from here! Get! Now!"

The coyote streaked away, its tail flying straight out behind it.

Helen stopped in her tracks, her body trembling so hard she could hardly hold the rifle. "Sadie, oh, Sadie!"

Sadie gently pulled the rifle from Helen. "It's gone. They're all gone, Helen."

Helen breathed deeply three times. She hid her trembling hands under her apron. "We did it, Sadie. We saved Bossie and Babe. And ourselves."

"We sure did, Helen." Sadie smiled as she gingerly rubbed her aching knee. "Let's get Bossie and Babe and go home." She turned and stopped dead in her tracks. "What in the world . . ."

A boy was leading Bossie away by her halter. For a minute she thought it was Web, but she could see the boy was taller, dressed in ragged dark pants and shirt. An old cap like Riley used to wear covered his head.

Anger and frustration rushed over Sadie, and she leaped forward and yelled, "Stop! Stop! Bring back our cow!"

2
More Trouble

"Bring back our cow!" cried Sadie as she ran faster. How dare someone steal Bossie, especially after they'd fought off coyotes to keep her!

Helen gasped and tried to catch up to Sadie. "Bring back our cow!" she echoed Sadie.

The boy looked back at them, then slapped Bossie on the rump and made her run. The calf bawled and kicked up its heels, then ran ahead of Bossie.

Sadie stopped short and gripped the rifle tighter. Her heart raced. "Stop! Stop or I'll shoot you!"

"Sadie, you can't shoot him," said Helen in alarm.

"Shh. He doesn't know that." Sadie raised the rifle to her shoulder. "Stop right now!"

"You won't shoot me," yelled the boy over his shoulder. "You might hit the cow." He kept running, with Bossie swaying beside him.

Sadie's head spun as she tried to think of a way to stop the thief. Finally she handed the rifle to Helen. "You hold this. I'm going to catch that boy and get Bossie back." She sounded more like Momma than herself.

"Don't let him hurt you." Trembling, Helen held the rifle as Sadie sped after the boy and Bossie.

Sadie raced after the boy just the way she'd run in school races back in Douglas County. Sometimes she'd even beat the big eighth-grade boys. She watched the gap close between her and the boy. She could see his dirty bare feet as he ran. Finally she leaped forward and tackled the boy around the legs. He lost his hold on the halter and slammed to the ground with Sadie on top of him. Sadie couldn't get her breath for a while, and the boy lay so still she wondered if she'd killed him. Then he shuddered, and she knew he was still alive. The boy's cap had fallen off, and Sadie saw dirty brown hair in a cut worse than Opal had ever given Web.

"Bossie's our cow and you can't take her," said Sadie in a low, tight voice.

The boy breathed hard and didn't answer.

Slowly Sadie stood up, her fists doubled at her sides. Her thin chest rose and fell. She smelled sweat. Her bonnet had fallen off her head and dangled down between her sharp shoulder blades. She glanced around to see that Bossie had stopped a couple of feet away. Babe ran to her and started sucking.

Helen ran to Sadie's side. "Is he dead?"

"No." Sadie nudged the boy's hard, bare foot with her toe. "Get up. What's wrong with you?"

Slowly the boy stood. His thin face was scratched and dirty, his blue eyes wide with fear and pain. "What're you gonna do with me?"

His speech was clipped and sounded strange to Sadie. "I should take you to York and tell him you tried to steal Bossie. He'd probably hang you."

"Sadie!" Helen stared at Sadie in alarm.

The boy bit his lip and rubbed his hands down his pants. "I won't do it again. Just let me go."

"Do your folks know what you're doin'?" snapped Sadie.

The boy scooped up his cap and clamped it on his head. "I got no folks."

"No folks? Are you an orphan?" asked Helen.

"I guess so."

Sadie frowned at Helen.

"Where do you live?" asked Helen.

The boy was quiet a long time. "On Cottonwood Creek."

"Jewel Comstock lives on Cottonwood Creek," said Sadie. "Do you know her?"

"I might."

"Her wagon team is a cow and a horse," said Helen.

The boy nodded. "I've seen her. She has a great big nose and a dog named Malachi that's as big as a horse."

"That's her," said Sadie. "Does she know you go around stealing cows from people?"

Sparks shot from the boy's blue eyes. "You gonna have me whipped or something?"

For some reason Sadie felt sorry for the boy. "You go back to your place and leave our cow alone and we won't tell anyone what you did."

The boy's thin shoulders sagged. "Don't do me no favors."

Sadie frowned. "Helen, get Bossie and let's go home."

Helen didn't move. "What's your name?" she asked the boy.

He chewed his lip. "Why'd you want to know?"

Helen shrugged. "I just do. I'm Helen and this is Sadie."

"Bob. Call me Bob," said the boy gruffly.

"I'm eight and Sadie is twelve. How old are you?"

"Twelve."

"Maybe we'll see you sometime when we're visiting Jewel," said Sadie.

"Don't count on it."

"Want to come eat dinner with us?" asked Helen.

Sadie could tell the boy longed to say yes, but he shook his head and rammed his hands deep into the pockets of his baggy pants.

"You could meet Momma and Opal and Web," said Helen. "Riley and York took biscuits with them when they rode out so they could finish fixin' the fence."

Just then Sadie saw a movement in the grass several feet away. "Quiet. I see a rabbit. I'll shoot it to take home." She aimed carefully and shot. The sound echoed over the vast prairie. The rabbit dropped in its tracks.

"You got it," said Helen in a weak voice. She hated to see animals get killed.

Bob shivered. "You're a good shot."

"Pretty good," said Sadie.

"You could've shot me a while ago."

"No!" cried Helen. "Sadie would never shoot any-one!"

Sadie saw the relief on Bob's face.

"I'll get the rabbit," said Bob. He ran to the rabbit, picked it up by the back legs so its head dangled down and blood ran to the ground. Instead of running back to them Bob held the rabbit high and shouted, "Thanks for dinner." He loped away, the dead rabbit swinging beside him.

"Come back here with that!" shouted Sadie.

"Don't steal our dinner!" cried Helen.

"I can't believe it," said Sadie, shaking her head.

"Aren't you gonna chase him and take back our rabbit?"

"No. Let him have it. We'll get something else on the way home."

Helen cupped her hands around her mouth and shouted after Bob, "You're a bad, bad boy!" She turned to Sadie. "There. I told him."

Sadie sighed. She watched until Bob was a tiny black speck on the prairie. "Let's go, Helen. Get Bossie."

Helen walked to Bossie and slipped her hand through the halter. "Come, Bossie. We're goin' home. And don't you run away again. I mean it. You made a lot of trouble for us today. And you almost got your calf ate by coyotes."

Sadie rubbed her sore knee, took a deep breath, and walked in the direction of the homestead. Since York had taught her to watch the shape of the hills to know directions she never got lost.

Helen glanced at Sadie. "Will anything else happen?"

"I hope not."

"I felt sorry for Bob."

"Me too."

"He's sad."

"I know."

"I saw it in his eyes. I thought he was gonna cry when I asked about his folks."

"He's an orphan," said Sadie. After Pa died she'd

felt like an orphan, even though she still had Momma and the family. "Maybe we should've made him go home with us."

"He wouldn't come to our house for dinner, but we gave him dinner anyway." Helen giggled and finally Sadie did too.

"Let's go home." The words seemed natural to Sadie. She'd thought it would take her forever to get used to living at the edge of the sandhills instead of in Douglas County, but now it was home. Momma and York were happily married. He'd never had a family before. He was an orphan, and the rancher who had found him under a cactus in Texas had named him York after the place in England where he'd lived. Now the whole family was called York instead of Merrill. Momma had said they all were getting a new start, and the new name went along with a new start.

Yesterday York had said he was ready to be given a first name. "Everyone else has two names," he'd said in his slow drawl with his wide-brimmed hat pushed to the back of his head. "Why shouldn't I? We'll all think about names for me, and then we'll give me a name. You young 'uns can call me Papa or Pa or Daddy if you want. But, Bess, I want you to call me by a first name and not York. It never bothered me before now, but it just don't seem right for a family man to be called one name. Give me a good, strong name and not some sissy one."

"What're you thinkin' about, Sadie?" Helen looked around Bossie's head at Sadie as they walked along.

"Givin' York a name."

"It's like namin' a new doll, and it takes a lot of thought." Momma had made Helen a rag doll for last Christmas, and she'd not found just the right name until almost the end of February. Finally she'd named the doll Naomi after Naomi in the Bible. Naomi had been dropped in the mud on the trip west and Helen had washed her carefully, but she didn't look the same. One button eye had come loose and Helen had sewed it on, but when she'd finished she'd realized it was lower than her other eye. She'd left it that way, hugged her close and said, "Naomi, don't let your eye bother you. I still love you."

Sadie shifted the rifle from her left hand to her right. "Opal made a list of Bible names. She tried to get me to side with her and call him David. I said I wouldn't."

"David's a nice name. Remember David Goos in our old school? He carried me through the snow one time so I could get inside without getting lost in a snowdrift."

"I heard Momma say that she liked Samuel, but would call him Sam. Web said to call him Levi, but I punched him and he stopped sayin' it." Levi was Pa's name, and it wouldn't be right to call York Levi. Besides, there was Levi Cass, the boy who had helped her with Tanner. Sadie smiled as she thought about Levi and her dog that had once belonged to mean Ty Bailer.

"Sometimes Web can be so dumb!" Helen pushed her bonnet off her head and let the wind dry the sweat on her scalp as she walked Bossie around the base of a hill. Babe ran back and forth beside them.

"A rabbit!" whispered Sadie.

Helen stopped, her hand tight on Bossie's halter.

Sadie aimed and fired, and the rabbit fell to the ground while the shot echoed. Sadie's heart leaped with excitement over hitting what she'd aimed at, but her stomach tightened as she thought about how happy the rabbit had been hopping over the grass.

"Poor bunny," said Helen.

Sadie ran to the rabbit and picked it up by its back legs. It felt limp and soft and warm. Blood drained from the spot just below the rabbit's eye where the bullet had hit. Blood splashed on her foot, and she wrinkled her nose. One rabbit wasn't enough to feed five people for dinner, but it would make a good gravy to eat over biscuits.

Helen pushed her face against Bossie's neck and walked away from the sight of the dead rabbit.

"You should be thankful I was able to get dinner," snapped Sadie, but she felt as badly as Helen.

They walked in silence for a long time, the wind blowing the grass, the birds singing, and Babe playing beside Bossie. Finally Helen looked up into the bright blue sky. "Thank You, God, for helping us get Bossie and Babe back."

Sadie nodded and mouthed, "Thank You, God."

3
Jewel's Visit

Sadie's jaw tightened and she gripped the rough hoe handle tighter as she heard York's laughter float from just outside the sod house to where she stood in the garden. How could he laugh after scolding Helen and Web so harshly over letting Bossie get away yesterday?

"He's not nice at all," she muttered as she chopped at a weed beside a tiny bean plant. "He's not even our real pa, and he scolds those kids like he is. And Momma lets him."

Sadie wanted to run to York and shake her finger at him and tell him just what she thought, but she knew Momma wouldn't allow her to do it. She knew York wouldn't either. To keep from bursting, she'd come to the garden to work after dinner instead of sitting in the yard laughing and talking with the others. For once York and Riley hadn't gone back to work, so it had seemed like a party except for Sadie's anger.

At the end of the row Sadie looked toward the house to see York swing Helen high in his arms. She giggled and hugged him. York's wide-brimmed hat fell to the ground. His damp, brown hair clung to his head where the hat brim had been. He was tall and lean and carried a Bowie knife on one hip and a Colt .45 on the other. He was three years younger than Momma and had never been married before. He'd first met Pa and Momma when he'd sold them a horse on one of his visits to eastern Nebraska. After Pa had died in the blizzard he'd stopped in, fell in love with Momma, and married her.

Helen giggled harder. Fresh anger rushed through Sadie. Why wasn't Helen mad at York? Web wasn't either. It didn't seem right.

Just then Tanner lifted his head and barked out into the prairie.

Sadie looked to see Jewel Comstock's wagon rolling across the grass toward them. It was easy to tell it was Jewel because a horse and a cow pulled the wagon as a team. A huge black dog, Malachi, padded alongside the cow.

Tanner barked, but didn't run out to meet them. Sadie had taught him to stay unless he had permission to go. He looked at Sadie, barked again, then settled down beside the barn to wait.

Having something exciting happen two days in a row was almost too much for Sadie. Part of the anger seeped out of her, and she reluctantly smiled. Maybe Jewel had heard about the orphan trying to steal Bossie. Sadie and Helen had told the story over and over to the family until Sadie was tired of it, but Helen told it with excitement each time even though she and Web had been scolded by York for not watching Bossie closer.

Helen was a born storyteller. Sadie liked to write her stories down, but she only had her slate to write on and she had to erase the story on it when it was time for lessons. The only paper in the house was for Momma to use to write her family in Michigan. Momma wrote tiny to fit as many words as possible on every inch of the paper. Sometimes she'd turn the paper sideways and write more across what she'd already written. Sadie thought it was hard to read, but Momma said she knew her family could read it. They were used to it by now.

Sadie thought about the friends she'd left behind in Douglas County, especially Emma White, and she wished she could write to them. She knew none of them expected letters from her, but she longed to hear from them. She wanted to know if Emma would be the best in spelling once school started again in September now that she was gone.

Jewel was close enough that Sadie could hear the creak of the wagon. She saw Momma pin back a strand of brown hair streaked with gray. Momma retied her apron around her sturdy body. Opal straightened her collar and brushed back the hair that had escaped her braids. Riley and Web stopped wrestling and waited beside York and Helen.

Sadie stood the hoe in place inside the sod barn, took a deep breath to let all of her anger rush out, then ran to join Momma and the others as they waited for Jewel to reach them.

Jewel was tall and broad and wore a man's wide-brimmed hat and heavy shoes. Her faded dress was covered with big patches of several pieces of different material. She was a lot older than Momma and had a voice that could be heard up into Dakota Territory.

"Brought you mail, Bess! Howdy, York, kids." Jewel's voice reached them before the team did. "I was in Jake's Crossing and the mail clerk said would I be goin' your way and I said I might be and he said you had mail. So here I am." She stopped the wagon and dropped from it before York could help her, wriggled her dress down to touch the tops of her big shoes, and held out a packet to Momma. "Here you go, Bess."

"Thank you." Momma looked at the three letters in her hand, her round face flushed with pleasure. Sadie wondered how Momma could hold the letters and not rip them open and read them, even if it was rude to do in front of company. This was the first mail Momma had received since Pa's funeral.

Jewel turned to Sadie and Opal. "I ran into Levi Cass, and he said he'd be stoppin' by too. He said he'd bring the mail, but I told him I wanted the privilege."

Levi Cass was coming!

Sadie's heart leaped. Jewel said something to York about the trip out, and Sadie glanced at Opal to see a pleased smile on her pretty face. Opal thought that someday she would marry Levi. Since they'd moved to the edge of the sandhills, he was the only fine young man Opal had met. Sadie hoped Opal would be ready to get married long before Levi would want to settle down with a wife. Sadie knew Levi planned to have a ranch of his own and raise cattle and horses like York did. He wouldn't be ready to take a wife in two years. And Opal wouldn't wait for him.

"It's good to see you, Jewel," said Momma in her soft voice the minute Jewel gave her a chance to speak. "Come in for a bite to eat."

"Be pleased to. But talk is what I want most." She smiled and for a minute drew attention to her pretty smile and away from her great hook of a nose.

"Did you hear about the orphan that tried to steal our cow?" asked Web. He stood with his hands tucked into the bib of his overalls. His blue eyes were as bright as the sky above.

Jewel pushed back her stained hat. "What's that you say?"

"Let me tell it," said Helen, stepping forward with her face beaming. The bright afternoon sun made her hair look fluffy-white.

"Are you sure you want to hear this?" asked Momma with a sigh.

"Why don't you have something to eat first?" asked York, standing with his hands resting lightly on his gun-belt.

"I want to hear everything," said Jewel. "It's been a long time since I had a chance to talk to a human being or listen to any news. I can eat any old time. Tell away, young lady." Jewel leaned against her wagon and folded her strong arms over her sagging breasts. Malachi lay at her feet and slapped his rope of a tail once, sending up a puff of dust.

Helen stood before Jewel as if she was reciting lessons in school. "It happened yesterday morning. I tied Bossie to the stake out there." Helen pointed, and Jewel looked to where she pointed. Bossie and Babe stood in the same spot. "I did tie the rope to Bossie's halter, but when I checked, the rope and the stake were there, but Bossie and Babe were gone. They weren't anywhere nearby. So Sadie and I went out lookin' for 'em."

Sadie glanced at York's sun-browned face, then looked quickly away to watch Jewel's team. The cow, Annie, chewed her cud and the horse, Ernie, stood with his head drooping. Was he ashamed of having a cow pull the wagon with him? Jewel had said they didn't know they weren't a normal team. When her mare had died, she'd taught Annie to pull with Ernie. Jewel had said she'd never told them the difference, so they didn't know they looked strange.

Annie moved restlessly and then slowly sank down to the ground to rest, chewing her cud the whole time. Ernie just stood there, his eyes drooping. Tanner sniffed them, but stayed away from Malachi.

When Helen finished, Jewel pulled off her hat, scratched her damp gray hair with a hand as tough as old leather, and said, "I'll be switched. I don't know of an orphan living on Cottonwood Creek. I know them two fellers bachin' in a dugout down from me. Bob, you say?"

"Bob," said Helen as if she'd created him.

"I'll have to keep a watch out for him." Jewel turned to Sadie. "You and your sister are brave girls fighting the coyotes that way. I couldn't have done better myself."

Sadie swelled with pride. "Thanks."

"They should've let me go with them," said Web. He still felt left out because they hadn't taken him. He'd wanted to face up to the dangerous coyotes. He'd wanted to fight the battle and have the story to tell. Instead he'd been left at home to hoe melons. He scowled at Sadie, but she shrugged and turned away. He hadn't expected her to understand, but he planned on being right there next time they went after coyotes or orphans.

Helen tossed her head. "We didn't need you."

Sadie waited until no one was looking at her or Web, and she jabbed him in the arm with her finger. "It's probably your fault Bossie got loose," she whispered.

"It's not! I told you that," he whispered back with a pained look on his thin face.

Sadie frowned at him and turned away. Both he and Helen had insisted that Bossie could not pull free from her rope. Did they think someone had actually untied her?

Had someone untied Bossie?

The thought rushed through Sadie and almost took her breath away. Maybe Bob had walked right up to Bossie and untied her so she'd walk away. Maybe he had even led her away.

Sadie knotted her fists and narrowed her dark eyes. If that was so, then York had scolded Helen and Web for no reason. Somehow she'd talk to Bob again and she'd find out the truth. If he had untied Bossie, Sadie would sure tell York a thing or two.

"How about lookin' at the gelding I told you about, Jewel?" York rested an arm lightly around Jewel's shoulders. She was almost as tall as he was.

"I can't pay you cash money," said Jewel, twisting the brim of her hat.

York shrugged. "After you have a bite to eat, we can take a ride out and see him. He's a fine gelding— gentle, but has a strong heart. You and Bess and me can ride out and look. We'll talk about what we can trade." York turned to Riley. "Water Annie and Ernie, then hitch up Dick and Jane and bring them around."

Riley with Web's help carried water to Annie and Ernie, while York, Momma, and Jewel walked inside the soddy with Jewel talking about what she could trade for the gelding.

Helen knelt down beside Malachi and circled his great neck with both her arms. "Do you want to hear all about the coyotes and the orphan?"

Sadie walked away to stand beneath Momma's tree that York had planted for her. It was the only tree in all of York's homestead, the only tree for miles and miles besides the few along Cottonwood Creek.

Sadie touched a leaf, then turned to see Opal beside her.

"I can't wait to see Levi," said Opal dreamily.

Sadie shrugged. She wanted to yell at Opal, but she forced back the bad words.

"I'm going to brush my hair and put on my shoes before he gets here." Opal touched her nutmeg-brown hair. Her blue eyes sparkled with excitement, and her cheeks were flushed a pretty pink. "I know he's coming to see me." She rubbed the toes of one small foot over the top of her other foot. "I think we'll go for a walk all by ourselves."

Sadie doubled her fists at her sides. "He's my friend too, and you can't take him off somewhere alone. I'll tell Momma on you if you even try!"

"Tattletale!"

"You're the one who's always tattling."

Opal widened her blue eyes innocently. "Me?"

"You told on me for spillin' the cream when I was churning."

"You were bein' careless!"

Sadie stepped right up to Opal. "I was not!"

"You were too!"

"I hope nobody ever wants to marry you!"

Opal flipped back her braids, but a stricken look crossed her face. "I will get married when I'm sixteen!"

"Not when you're sixteen or sixty! Never! Old maid!" The hateful words leaped out of Sadie's mouth before she could stop them. Those were the words she always used when she wanted to hurt Opal deeply. How could she be so mean to Opal? She wanted to grab back the words, but it was too late.

Opal whirled around and ran to the barn to be alone and weep over the possibility of being an old maid.

Sadie sank to the ground. Tanner licked her cheek, but she didn't feel any better.

4

Sadie's Good Dress

Sadie watched Dick and Jane pull York's wagon away from the yard toward the pasture where York kept his horses. Momma and York sat on the seat, and Jewel and Riley sat behind them with Malachi running along beside. Riley had asked to go along. Sadie knew it was because he didn't much care for Levi. Riley knew Levi thought of him as a farmer and not a rancher, and Riley didn't like that at all.

Tanner whined and pawed Sadie's foot.

"What's the matter, boy?" Sadie rubbed Tanner's ears and patted his brown coat. He waved his tail and licked her arm. "Did you want to go? You stay here with me. Levi will want to see how big you've grown in the last two weeks."

Sadie brushed an ant off her skirt and then noticed just how worn and old her dress looked. How could she let Levi see her in such an old dress? Opal wasn't the only one who could make herself pretty for company. Sadie took a step toward the house.

"Where are you goin', Sadie?" asked Helen as she hung the dipper in place after getting a drink of cold well water.

Sadie flipped back her braids. "To change my dress."

"Oh!" Helen ran to Sadie's side and stared up at her. "You know you aren't supposed to wear your good dress except for goin' to town. Momma said so."

"Levi's comin' and I won't let him see me in this old dress." Sadie rubbed her hand over a new tear.

"He saw you in it before."

"But look how dirty it is. Look at the patch I had to sew on it." Sadie rubbed her hand over the big patch that she'd slip-stitched over a ragged rip in the material. It was right in plain sight just to the side of her apron.

"What about your other everyday dress?"

"It's in the wash. I spilled cream on it." Sadie wrinkled her nose at the thought of the sour smell on her other dress. She'd rinsed it out before she'd tossed it in the pile of dirty clothes, but it had still smelled.

She owned three dresses, two calico and one gingham. Two were for everyday and one was for good. The good dress once had been Opal's, but she'd grown too tall for it and so Momma had hemmed it to fit Sadie. Sadie frowned. She was the runt of the family. Web was almost as tall as she, and he was only nine. One of her greatest dreams was to grow bigger than Opal, so she wouldn't be able to wear Opal's hand-me-downs.

Just then Opal walked from the soddy. She wore her good dress, new bonnet, and her shoes. She looked so beautiful that Sadie wanted to slap her. She lifted her small chin and looked around daintily. "Is he here yet?"

35

"No!" snapped Sadie.

Helen twisted her apron around her hands. "Sadie's gonna put on her good dress."

Sadie scowled at Helen, then faced Opal defiantly. "You put yours on, so why can't I?"

"Because you're too careless, Sadie Rose York!"

"I am not!"

"Momma told you your good dress has to last for a long time and that you have to take extra good care of it."

Sadie tossed her head. "I will take good care of it. I'm gonna put it on and wear it, and you can't stop me."

Opal shook her head. "I'll tell Momma."

"She's not here."

"When she gets back."

"See if I care!"

Helen caught at Sadie's hand. "Don't do anything to make Momma spank you again." It hurt Helen almost as much to see Sadie or Web spanked as it did to get spanked herself.

Sadie doubled her fists and stamped her foot. Dust puffed up. "I will wear my good dress and I won't ruin it and I won't get spanked!" Momma had told her two days ago that she really was getting too grown-up to be spanked. She'd been spanked only one time in all of this year. Momma wouldn't spank her just because she wanted to look nice for company.

A few minutes later Sadie stood at Momma's looking glass to see how she looked. Her dark hair hung in new braids, with no strands of hair straggling out on her face. She touched the smooth sleeve and rubbed a hand down her skirt. The dress was a blue gingham and it fit loose, but it was nicer than her everyday dress. Momma had made the dress for Opal before Pa had died, but the blue was almost as bright as it had been when it was brand-new. Sadie's shoes pinched her feet, but it was worth it to look nice for Levi.

"I look good," she whispered, then flushed that she dared to be so vain. She glanced toward the door to make sure no one had heard her, then she walked outdoors. Wind pushed her skirt against her thin legs and flattened the ruffles of her bonnet against her forehead.

Was it really worth getting all dressed up for Levi Cass?

She shrugged and nodded. Levi might pay more attention to her than to Opal if she didn't look ragged and boyish.

Bossie bawled, and Sadie glanced toward her. Helen held the rope and stake and led Bossie to a new grazing spot. Babe leaped and danced and followed. Helen pounded the stake down deep into the sandy ground, patted Bossie, and ran back to the yard. York had said that soon he'd be able to buy barbed wire to make a fence for Bossie and Babe; then they wouldn't have to stake Bossie out. He had a stack of fence posts waiting that he'd bought when he'd sold a horse. Riley had started digging the post holes, but it took a long time. He did it without complaining because he knew it was just another chore a rancher had to do.

Helen looked at Sadie a long time. "Maybe I better put on my good dress."

"Don't you dare!"

"I can do it if you can."

"You cannot!" Sadie shook her finger at Helen. "I just finished putting in the hem of your new dress, and I won't let you wear it and rip it or get it dirty."

Helen skipped toward the barn and called over her shoulder, "I don't want to wear it anyway. I can't play with it on."

Sadie sighed long and deep. Helen was right. Sadie

37

retied her sash and sighed again. Maybe she should change. Then she caught sight of Opal walking away from the outhouse and shook her head. She couldn't change, not with Opal all dressed up.

Listlessly Sadie walked to the well, filled the dipper with cold water, and drank. The water slipped down her dry throat and tasted good. York said they had the best water in the world.

She hung the dipper in place and scanned the prairie for Levi. He usually rode his mare when he came. She watched a jackrabbit stand tall, look around, then bound away. Birds swayed on grasses. The wind was in the wrong direction to hear York's windmill squawk as it turned to pump water into the big tank for the cattle and horses. York had said soon he'd have a windmill in the yard for them. He'd also said he could soon start building onto the house to make a bigger sod house so they'd all fit. Sadie wanted a frame house like they'd lived in in Douglas County, but York couldn't afford to buy the lumber yet.

Sadie watched Opal spread a quilt under the tree and sit down as if she was a picture from one of Momma's books. Sadie doubled her fists and turned quickly away.

Tanner barked frantically from the other side of the sod barn, and Sadie ran to see what was wrong. She stopped short.

A rattlesnake lay several feet in front of her, tasting the air with its long tongue.

Web and Helen shouted and laughed as they each straddled a hoe, riding the hoes as their horses. They were heading right for the rattlesnake.

Sadie tried to call to them, but her throat closed over and no sound came out.

Perspiration popped out on her forehead. Her

good dress suddenly felt burning hot against her slight body. She glanced at Tanner to see that he was crouching as if he'd spring at the snake if it made a wrong move.

Just then Web spotted Sadie. "See my horse!" He leaped high, waving his left arm in the air while he gripped his horse just under the head of the hoe.

"Mine too!" shouted Helen, giggling.

Sadie opened her mouth and finally pushed out, "Stop! A rattlesnake."

Web and Helen stopped dead, and Sadie could tell when they spotted the snake by the way they tensed. Slowly they pulled their hoes from between their legs and held them as weapons.

"Bring me your hoe, Helen," said Sadie in a tight voice. She held out her hand.

Before Helen could move, the snake turned and slithered toward Sadie. Slowly she lowered her hand, her heart thudding so loud she was sure even Opal could hear it.

The snake stopped and tasted the air again.

"We'll kill it," said Web in a voice that sounded like Riley's at his most confident.

Sadie held her breath and watched as Web and Helen inched their way forward toward the snake. The snake coiled, and a chill ran over Sadie's body. Silently she prayed for help from God.

After years of practice by chopping a weed without hitting a valuable plant, Web struck with his hoe and sliced into the snake just back of its head. Helen chopped down and sliced into the middle of its body. Web lifted his hoe and chopped down again and again and again.

"We got it," said Helen, her face as white as the clouds in the sky.

"I think we killed it," said Web, his voice shaking almost as much as his arms.

Sadie stepped closer, her heart racing. She looked down at the huge snake. Its head was chopped almost off, and several places along its body were sliced through. "I guess it is dead."

"We got it," said Helen again, holding the hoe as a weapon over the snake in case it moved again.

Tanner whined, but stayed back.

"I'll cut off the rattles for York," said Web, but he didn't move.

York kept the rattles of all the rattlesnakes he'd killed inside his guitar. He liked to tell about how he'd killed each one. Sometimes Web would shake them out of the hole in the guitar and hold them and count them and pretend he'd killed the snakes himself.

The snake twitched, and Helen and Web yelped and jumped back. Tanner barked. Sadie's legs shook so much, she thought she'd fall right on the snake.

"Give me your hoe, Helen," said Sadie.

Slowly Helen held it out.

Sadie's hand closed around the rough wood, hot from Helen's hands. Sadie swallowed hard, then carefully lifted the snake with the hoe. It was heavy and took all of her strength to hold it up. It slipped off and fell in a heap. Sadie shivered and lifted the snake again. "It's dead." She dropped it down and worked it out into a long line. It was at least three feet long and as big around as Helen's wrist. "I'll hold its head down while you cut off the rattle, Web."

"I can't watch," said Helen, but she kept her eyes glued to the snake.

Web handed his hoe to Helen, pulled out his knife, opened it, and bent down to the snake. The color drained from his face. He wanted to turn and run, but he also wanted to be able to brag to everyone that he'd cut off the rattles. He lifted the tail, forced back a shiver, and cut off the rattles in one easy cut. He jumped back with a great laugh and shook the rattles. Tanner barked.

"You did it," said Helen in awe. She gingerly touched the rattles. "I would've been too afraid."

"I wasn't scared at all!" Web shook the rattles again.

Sadie carried the snake on the hoe to the fence around the garden and hung it over it. Some people said it would rain if you hung a snake on a fence, but she didn't believe that.

The snake dangled limply, then jerked, and Sadie leaped back. Tanner barked and jumped up on her, his big paws on her waist.

She remembered her good dress and she looked in horror at the great paws touching her precious dress. "Down, boy!" She pushed against his broad chest.

Tanner's toenail caught in a gather at Sadie's waist. She heard a loud rip, and her heart dropped. All the color drained from her face, and the strength oozed from her body.

Frantically she caught at Tanner's paw to keep him from tearing her dress all the way to the hem. Carefully she worked the toenail free and let him drop to the ground. He cringed at her feet as if he knew he'd done a terrible thing.

"My dress!" she mouthed. Inside she was shouting, "My only good dress! It's ruined! My dress! What will Momma say?"

Sadie shot a look at Helen and Web. They were engrossed in the rattle and didn't notice what had happened.

Oh, what should she do?

She had to get the dress off before anyone saw the tear.

She spun around away from Web and Helen and looked across the prairie for signs of Momma coming back. Only a hawk flew in the sky, and Bossie and Babe moved on the prairie.

Tanner whined at her feet as if he was apologizing.

She walked away from him, her heart in her tight shoes, her stomach a cold, hard knot.

"Momma will be so mad," whispered Sadie, blinking back tears.

5
Levi's Visit

Sadie touched the tear in her dress, then wiped the sweat off her face with the back of her hand.

"Web, let's show Opal the rattle," said Helen, giggling as she danced around Web.

"I get to tell her what happened," said Web, looking proud.

Helen lifted her chin high. "I can tell it better!"

"But it's my turn! You got to tell about the orphan and the coyotes!"

Helen shrugged. "Oh, all right."

Sadie waited until they ran around the house to the tree, then dashed to the sod house and slipped inside. She stood in the darkness of the soddy, trembling with tears burning her eyes. Fumbling with the buttons, she finally pulled off her good dress and changed back into her everyday dress.

Her world was ruined, but bright afternoon sun-light still streamed in the door. It was quickly swallowed up by the thick sod walls. With the fire in the cookstove out, the room was pleasantly cool. The aroma of coffee hung in the air from Momma, York, and Jewel having coffee before they drove out to the pasture.

Sadie touched the long rip in her good dress. It was too awful to be real, but it wasn't a nightmare.

She peeked out the door. She heard Web talking, but there was no sign of York's wagon.

Her hand trembling, Sadie set Momma's sewing basket on the table so she could see from the light from the window. She found blue thread and a needle. As long as she could remember, Momma had had the big woven sewing basket that held several spools of thread, buttons, needles, three silver thimbles, and a crochet hook made of bone.

After the fourth try Sadie threaded the needle, knotted the thread, and held the needle over the soft gingham material.

From outdoors she heard the rattle of harness and creak of a wagon.

"Momma!"

The needle fell from her fingers to the floor. Sadie dropped to her knees to find it. Frantically she searched the bare dirt floor that she'd swept just hours ago. She had to put the sewing basket back before Momma walked in and caught her.

Finally she found the needle, unthreaded it, and stuck it back in place. She wrapped the thread back around the spool. She knew she dare not waste even a few inches of thread. Quickly she set the sewing basket back on Momma's chest of drawers and hung her dress behind Helen's on the peg that York had put up special for dresses. She fixed it so the tear wouldn't show, dropped her shoes back in the trunk, and ran to the door.

She squared her thin shoulders and walked into the bright afternoon sunlight, then stopped short just outside the door.

Levi with Opal beside him was walking toward the barn, with Helen chattering to him. Web carried a bucket of water to a team of horses that stood near the well. Levi hadn't ridden his mare Netty.

Momma wasn't home after all.

Sadie let out her breath in one long sigh, then scowled. Levi was here and no one had called her. Levi hadn't sought her out. Maybe he didn't want to be friends any longer.

Tears stung her eyes, and she bit her bottom lip until the tears faded away.

She could've mended the tear in her dress! Now it was too great of a risk. Besides, she wanted to see Levi.

Sadie ran to Web. "I'll finish watering the horses, Web."

"Thanks!" He'd wanted to be with Levi and Opal when they saw the terrible snake hanging on the fence.

Sadie watched Web run around the barn after the others, then she patted first one horse and then the other on their sleek necks. The horses moved restlessly, and their harness rattled. Sadie glanced back in the wagon, then looked closer. A mule deer lay on its side, its legs out stiff in death, its huge ears high, its insides gutted out.

Just then Helen skipped across the yard toward Sadie. "Web wouldn't let me tell any of the snake story, so I came to look at the dead deer again."

"Where's Levi?"

"Hangin' on everything Opal says." Helen rolled her eyes. "I'd rather look at the dead deer." She climbed up the wheel and hung over the wagon. "Look at that eye. Just starin' at us. Looks like a giant marble. Remember the marbles David Goos had back where we used to live?"

Sadie frowned down at the deer. She hated looking at its eye.

"Levi brought it to us to eat. He said his Paw told him to since he was comin' anyway."

Sadie tugged on Helen's skirt. "Why didn't you tell me Levi was here?"

"I don't know."

"Did he ask about me?"

"No."

Sadie's shoulders drooped, and she stared down at her bare feet. "Didn't he even wonder where I was?"

"He looked around and he said he thought you'd be here and Opal said you were and he didn't say nothin' else about you. She asked him about the deer, and he told her how he shot it right in the brain with one shot." Helen dropped to the ground and pushed back her thin, white braids. "It sounded like he was braggin', but I guess not. I don't think Levi Cass would brag. Do you?"

"He might." Sadie looked toward the barn. "I might just walk over there and see what's goin' on."

Helen stepped right up beside Sadie. "I might walk with you."

"It wouldn't be right if I didn't speak to Levi after he came all this way."

Helen looked at Sadie, glanced away, then looked again. "You changed your dress, Sadie. How come?"

Sadie locked her suddenly icy hands behind her back. "I wanted to. Anything wrong with that?"

"No. Momma won't get mad now."

Sadie shot a look toward the open prairie for sight

of Momma. Momma's hen and her chicks were scratching for worms, but no wagon was in sight. Sadie breathed easier. Somehow she'd have to find a way to make some cash money to buy a length of fabric for a dress. She might as well wish Pa would come down from Heaven, jump back inside his body, and start living again.

"What're you waitin' on, Sadie?"

"Nothin'." Sadie walked toward the barn with Helen half-running beside her. Abruptly Sadie stopped and caught Helen's arm. "Do I look all right? Is my face dirty?"

Helen looked at her questioningly. "You look fine to me."

"Are you sure?"

Helen shrugged.

Suddenly Sadie turned and ran back to the house. She wasn't looking for a fine young man to marry like Opal was. She wouldn't act like Opal around Levi or any other boy.

Helen stopped in the doorway beside Sadie. "What're you gonna do, Sadie?"

"Nothin'!"

"I thought you wanted to talk to Levi."

"I changed my mind."

"Your face is clean."

Sadie tossed her head. "I have work to do. If Levi wants to talk to me, he can come find me."

"Should I tell him that?"

Sadie gripped Helen's thin arm. "No! Don't you dare!"

"Ouch!" Helen squirmed free and rubbed her arm. "What's wrong with you, Sadie?"

"Nothin'! Not one thing!"

A dog barked, and Sadie stepped outdoors to see

47

Malachi running in front of York's wagon. Sadie pressed her hand against the pulse in her throat. For sure it was too late to mend her dress now. She'd have to find a way to mend it without Momma knowing. Someday she'd tell Momma about the tear. Just maybe she could mend it so well that nobody would be able to see her tiny stitches.

She shook her head slightly. The stitches would show no matter how careful she was. Somehow she'd have to find the courage to tell Momma what had happened. But not today and not until she absolutely had to.

Maybe a miracle would happen and a mouse would chew up her good dress and Momma would never learn about the tear.

Just then Levi, Opal, and Web ran to the yard to wait for York's wagon. The rumble of the wagon grew louder. Jewel's laugh boomed out.

Levi stepped to Sadie's side. He wore a blue shirt with a red paisley neckerchief tied around his neck. He smiled, and his white teeth flashed in his dark face. "Howdy."

Sadie looked him right in the eye, but didn't smile. "Hello."

"I brought you all a deer." He looked proud of himself.

"That's nice."

His smile faded. "I shot it with one shot."

She lifted her chin a fraction. "I shot a rabbit with one shot."

"Oh." He moved from one booted foot to another.

York jumped from the wagon and helped Momma down, while Riley jumped out and helped Jewel down. All the while Jewel talked more than Helen ever had.

"I'm not used to bein' helped none," said Jewel,

48

shaking her patched dress down to her huge shoes. She lifted a hand to Levi. "I see you made it."

"Sure did."

York looked in Levi's wagon. "What's this you have here?"

"A mule deer," said Web. "Levi shot it with one shot right in the brain!"

"Paw wants you to have it," said Levi to York.

"Thank your paw for us," said York. "Riley, take it to the barn and hoist it up so we can skin it."

"I'll help," said Web.

"Me too," said Levi. He glanced at Sadie, but still she didn't smile. He jumped in the wagon and drove the team to the barn.

For the first time Sadie noticed Opal standing beside her.

"I'm tellin' Momma you were rude to Levi," whispered Opal.

Sadie's jaw tightened. "Go right ahead and tell her. I'll tell her you pinched your cheeks to make 'em pink."

Opal's blue eyes that were so much like Pa's grew big and round. "I did no such thing!"

Sadie hung her head in shame. "I know you didn't."

"Then why did you say I did?"

Sadie shrugged. She knew why, but she couldn't put it into words.

Just then York strode to Sadie and clamped his hand on her shoulder. She smelled his sweat and the leather smell that always seemed part of him. "Sadie Rose, I need you to do something for Jewel."

Sadie looked up into York's sun-browned face. Laugh-lines spread from the corners of his blue eyes into the brown and gray hair under his sweat-stained, wide-brimmed hat. He always called her Sadie Rose, no matter that she'd told him that everyone called her only by her first name. "What do you want me to do?"

York bent down until his face was close to Sadie's. "Go home with her and give her a hand a couple of days. She'll be leavin' directly."

"But . . . but . . ." Sadie glanced toward the barn where Levi was unloading the deer with Riley. "Right now? You want me to go right now?"

"Sure do. Jewel's pickin' up a couple wagon loads of cow chips, and I told her you'd be glad to help."

Sadie glanced at Jewel who was talking to Momma about baking bread, then looked up at York. "I don't want to go," she said in a low voice that neither Jewel nor Momma could hear.

York pushed his hat back and rubbed a hand over his jaw. "I reckon you don't have a choice, Sadie Rose. She needs you, and I said you'd go."

Angry words leaped into Sadie's mouth, but she swallowed them. She knew she couldn't talk back to York. "Could . . . could Opal go instead?"

"Me?" cried Opal.

"Your momma depends too much on Opal." York looped his thumbs under his gunbelt and studied Sadie for a long time.

Finally Sadie nodded. She knew she had to obey.

"Helen," called Jewel. "Tell the boys to bring my team and wagon, would you, darlin'?"

Sadie's heart sank as Helen dashed away. She wouldn't have a chance to talk further to Levi. She'd have to leave him with Opal and her big blue eyes and pink cheeks.

"Take your shoes just in case and a change of clothes along with your night things," said York. "Get ready. Don't be long."

Sadie barely nodded. When York walked away, she

ran into the house and grabbed her nightdress and a change of underclothes. She lifted her shoes out of the trunk where all the shoes were kept so mice wouldn't gnaw on them. She'd have to take her dirty dress that smelled of sour cream. Tomorrow she'd wash it in Cottonwood Creek and dry it on the ground.

She stared at the peg that held her good dress, took a deep, quivering breath, turned, and walked out with her clothes bundled together.

Momma hugged her and said, "See you in two days, Sadie. Be good for Jewel. Mind her well."

Sadie climbed in the wagon beside Jewel while the others said good-bye. She didn't hear Levi's voice, and she wouldn't look at him. She kept her eyes glued to Annie and Ernie as they pulled the wagon out into the vast prairie.

6

The Ride to Jewel's

The hot afternoon sun burned through Sadie's bonnet as she watched Annie swish her rope of a tail. She heard Malachi panting in the wagon just in back of Jewel.

"Why the long face?" asked Jewel. "It's not too late for me to turn around and take you back."

Sadie pulled her sunbonnet forward to hide more of her face. "I want to help you, Jewel." She really did too. It's just that she hated leaving Levi after she'd been so mean to him the few minutes that they'd had together. Now Opal would have an even greater advantage.

Jewel tucked her dress between her knees with one big hand and held the reins lightly with the other. "Did I ever tell you I was one of the first babies to be born in Nebraska?"

"Yes."

"Oh, yes. I did, didn't I? You and your brothers and sisters were born in Nebraska too."

"But we didn't live in the oldest settlement like you did."

"And your pa never had to fight Indians like mine did." Jewel glanced at the rifle stuck in the special boot at the side of her wagon, right in easy reach if she needed it fast.

Sadie touched a pile of sand with her bare toe. "Pa almost had to fight in the War Between the States. He was just ready to enlist and it was over. That was before he and Momma were married. Momma told us about it."

"My pa once kept an escaped Negro family in our barn overnight so they could rest before they went farther west."

Sadie smoothed the patch on her dress. "I never saw a Negro person before. Are they like we are?"

"I reckon. Just different colored skin."

Sadie thought about that a long time. "Indians have different colored skin."

"Negroes are darker." Jewel pulled back on the reins. "Whoa, Annie, Ernie."

Her brows cocked, Sadie glanced at Jewel.

"I see a hefty supply of buffalo chips in the area. We might as well pick 'em up since we got enough daylight left. Buffalo grazed these parts a few years ago. There were herds and herds of them, and I still find plenty of chips to pick up. All dried, too. Don't have to worry none about fresh ones like when you pick up cow chips." Jewel sprang from the wagon with Malachi beside her. "I watched my pa skin a buffalo once. I still got the robe he made from the hide."

Sadie jumped to the ground, lifted a basket from the back of the wagon that Jewel carried especially for picking up chips, and walked toward the area that was heavy with dried manure. Grass tickled her bare feet and ankles.

A prairie dog barked a warning, and all the others shot into their homes out of sight. Malachi barked once, but didn't bother trying to catch one.

With the warm wind blowing her skirts tight against her, Sadie filled her basket, dumped it in the back of the wagon in a heap, and walked back to fill it again.

Birds sang. Ernie nickered. Then the only sound for a minute was the wind.

Jewel talked about burning chips and twisting hay to burn while she filled her basket. Sometimes Sadie could hear her well and other times when Jewel bent to the ground, her voice got muffled and Sadie couldn't hear, but she didn't tell. She knew Jewel was glad to have someone to talk to, even if they couldn't hear every word. Usually she had only Malachi.

After almost an hour of gathering chips, Jewel called Sadie back to the wagon. "I reckon we got to get home and do the chores before dark."

Thankfully Sadie sat on the wagon seat. Pain shot through her lower back, but she didn't let Jewel know. Jewel slapped the reins on Ernie's and Annie's backs and told them to giddap. Sadie pulled off her bonnet and let the warm wind dry her damp hair. Her braids bobbed on her shoulders from the jostling of the wagon. Her mouth was dry and she longed for a drink, but she knew she'd have to wait until they reached Jewel's place.

"I'll be switched," said Jewel.

"What?" asked Sadie.

"I think I just saw your orphan."

Sadie gripped the seat and gazed around. All she

saw was rolling hills and birds flying in the blue sky. "Where?"

"My eyes could be playin' tricks on me, but I sure thought I saw someone right over there between them two blowouts."

"I don't see anything."

"We'll check it out." Jewel slapped the reins against Annie and Ernie. "Get up, Annie, Ernie."

Ernie ran with Annie swaying her funny cow run beside him. Sadie held on tight to the seat and braced her feet against the rough floor.

Suddenly the right back end of the wagon dropped, and the team jerked to a stop. Sadie pitched forward, then flipped back and landed on the buffalo chips, her feet in the air and her skirts around her waist. Ernie whinnied, and Annie bellered as if she was hurt.

Sadie struggled to her feet to find Jewel lying half in and half out of the wagon. Her hat had fallen to the ground. Sadie gripped Jewel's arm and tugged her to the seat. "Are you all right?"

"I think so." Jewel rubbed her side and whistled softly. "That was a mighty big jolt." Jewel looked back. "The wheel fell off. We can thank God we weren't hurt." She climbed to the ground with a groan. She rubbed her hip, then picked up her hat and smashed it in place on her damp gray hair. Malachi whined up at her as if he was asking if she was hurt. She patted his head. "I'm just fine, Malachi."

Sadie scrambled to the ground and looked down at the wheel. "The nut fell off."

"Do you see it?"

Sadie searched in the grass around the wagon, then backtracked a few feet. Her heart sank. "No sign of it."

Jewel sighed heavily, studied the sun a minute, then

patted Malachi's great head. "We'll have to go back and look until we find it." She walked around to Annie and Ernie, patted them and talked to them to calm them, then pulled her rifle from its boot. "Let's go. Come, Malachi."

"Should I stay with the wagon?" Sadie trembled at the idea of being out in the middle of the prairie all alone.

Jewel frowned in thought, then shook her head. "We'd best stick together, Sadie girl. You and me better. You and me and Malachi."

Sadie fell into step beside Jewel. Her feet looked tiny next to Jewel's shoes that probably had belonged to her dead husband.

A hawk screeched in the sky, swooped down, and caught a young rabbit in its talons, then flew out of view.

Sadie shuddered.

"I wouldn't want to be that little rabbit. With a nose like mine, not even a hawk would want me." Jewel laughed and patted her hook of a nose. "I once was quite a beauty. Except for my nose, of course. Eli didn't care about my nose. He married me anyway." Jewel looked down the path the wagon had taken as if she was looking back into her past. "In those days, and these too I reckon, there weren't many girls to choose from. A man settled for what he could get. But me and Eli had a good life. A good life."

"Do you get lonely livin' all alone in your dugout?"

"Sure do. But I got Malachi here."

"Maybe you could get that orphan to live with you."

"He wouldn't want to be stuck with an old woman like me." Jewel's voice sounded wistful, and Sadie knew Jewel would like to share her place with another human.

Just then Sadie spotted the nut. It lay in a greasy heap next to a prickly pear. She picked it up carefully, but grease rubbed into her hand anyway.

"Glad you found it, Sadie. We'll get it on and be on our way." Jewel rubbed Malachi's small ears. "She found it, Malachi. We're gonna be all right now."

"How can we get the wheel back on?" asked Sadie as they walked back toward the wagon that she could see standing like a big dot on the prairie. She knew how heavy the wagon was. She'd watched York and Riley together struggle with a bar as a lever to lift the axle high enough to slip a wheel in place.

Jewel pulled off her hat and rubbed her head. "Now that's a puzzler." She looked up at the sky. "Heavenly Father, You see us and our predicament. Show us what to do, would You?"

Sadie squirmed uneasily as she stared down at the greasy nut. She didn't want God to look down at her right now, not until she had it all settled about her torn dress, her meanness to Levi and Opal, and her anger at York.

But York had said her Heavenly Father was always with her. Then He would already know about the bad things she'd done.

She pushed that terrible thought away as they reached the wagon. She carefully laid the nut on the ground beside the axle, then lifted the wheel and rested it against the wagon.

Jewel pushed her rifle back in place. "We found the nut. God'll show us what to do." She looked at the wheel and the nut and then out into the prairie as if she expected someone to ride up to help her. "You're a worker of miracles, Father God, and we need a miracle right now."

Just then Sadie saw a cloud of dust on the horizon,

and her heart stood still. Was God sending someone to help them? Was He really answering?

A herd of deer ran past close enough that Sadie could see their long ears. She sighed in relief. She just couldn't have God paying any attention to her right now. She and Jewel would have to figure out for themselves how to get the wheel back on.

Jewel walked around to pat Annie and Ernie. "Don't you two worry none about this. God'll answer. He always does."

Sadie held her breath and looked around again. She gasped and froze in her spot. A rider was coming toward them on a giant white horse.

Was it God Himself?

She trembled and felt a sob rising inside her.

"Thank You, Father!" shouted Jewel, swinging her hat high. "I knew You wouldn't fail me."

Sadie sank to the ground with her back against the wagon. She wanted to crawl out of sight, but there was nowhere to go.

Malachi barked as if he knew the rider.

"It's Carl White on Marengo! He's one of them bachelor boys that live up the creek from me. From Switzerland, he is. That's a far piece from here. Came over on a boat, he said."

Sadie's breath swooshed back into her body, and weakly she stood to her feet. It wasn't God Himself. But God had answered and sent someone to help them. Her legs trembled.

"Howdy, Carl!" shouted Jewel. "You're a sight for sore eyes, son!"

Sadie watched as Carl rode closer. She could see he was one of the fine young men that Opal was always looking for. He was probably in his twenties and he wore chaps and boots like York, a plaid shirt, and a big white hat that shadowed his eyes.

"Howdy, Jewel, Malachi." Carl slid out of the saddle and dropped the reins to dangle on the ground. He was taller and broader than York, but younger. He pushed his hat to the back of his head, and Sadie saw the twinkle in his dark eyes. "What's goin' on here? Run into trouble, did you?"

He talked with a strange accent, but Sadie could understand him without any problem. She stepped away from the wagon, and he glanced at her and his dark brows shot up.

"Who's the little one, Jewel? You get yourself a family, did you?"

Jewel laughed her great bark of a laugh. "York's girl, Carl. Sadie York, Carl White."

Carl pulled off his hat and bowed slightly, and Sadie flushed to the roots of her dark hair. He walked toward her, his chaps flapping against his strong legs. Dust covered the toe of his boots. "I'm glad to meet York's girl. I'm pleased to meet you, Sadie."

Sadie couldn't say a word. She nodded slightly, but that's all she could manage.

"A wheel came off, Carl," said Jewel, motioning to the wheel. "You're an answer to prayer, you are. Could you give us a hand?"

"Be pleased to." He laid his white hat on the wagon seat, then bent down. "I'll lift it enough for you to slip the wheel on, then we'll ease the wheel back in place."

Jewel lifted the wheel to the axle. "You and me could lift and Sadie could slip it on, Carl."

"I can do it. Wouldn't want you to hurt yourself." He glanced at her. "Ready?"

"Ready."

Sadie twisted her fingers in her skirts as she watched Carl White strain under the weight of the wagon. Muscles rippled under his shirt. The wagon creaked, and Jewel maneuvered the wheel onto the end of the axle. With a grunt Carl lifted it higher, and Jewel pushed the wheel into position. Carl turned the nut and stepped back with a pleased nod.

"That takes care of that," he said. He rubbed his greasy hands onto the grass, then wiped them on a handkerchief from his back pocket.

"That was a fine piece of work, Carl," said Jewel. "You stop by my place for supper anytime and I'll feed you a good meal. You bring Sven with you. He's nothin' but a toothpick, so he could stand a meal."

"Thanks." Carl clamped his hat in place and winked at Sadie. "Are you always this quiet?"

"Usually," she whispered.

"You're about the size of that thievin' orphan I was after."

Sadie gasped. "Did you see the orphan? A ragged boy? So did I! He almost stole our cow!"

"You don't say."

"What'd he take from you?" asked Jewel.

"Food. We got supplies in yesterday, and he took some of them today. I thought I spotted him a while ago when I was looking for a steer that got away from us."

With a dirty hand Sadie shielded her eyes against the sun and looked toward the blowouts where Jewel had thought she'd seen the orphan.

7

The Missing Dress

Sadie sloshed her dress up and down in the bucket of cold water from Cottonwood Creek. Momma would frown at that. She said nothing came clean unless it was washed in boiling hot water. Momma kept a special stick to push the clothes down under the boiling water so they wouldn't scald their hands.

Sadie wrinkled her nose at the smell of the lye soap Jewel had told her to use as she rubbed it into the cotton material. Birds sang in the two cottonwood trees beside the creek that shaded the area to Jewel's dugout. The water rippled along over the sandy creek bottom.

Sadie rinsed her dress and flung the water out across the grass. Warm wind blew sprinkles of water back against her. She filled the bucket with more water and rinsed the dress again. She heard Jewel talking to Malachi near her sod barn. Annie and Ernie grazed in the corral. Earlier Sadie had milked Annie while Jewel fed her chickens.

Sadie squeezed the water out of the dress, then spread it out over the sweet-smelling grass where the sun would dry it by the time they got back from picking up buffalo chips. A fly buzzed around her head, and she swatted it away.

At the edge of the corral Jewel called, "Annie, Ernie, it's time to go."

While Jewel hitched the team to the wagon, Sadie ran into the dugout, picked up the cotton "sugar sack" of fried chicken and biscuits they'd packed for dinner along with the jug of water, ran to the wagon, and climbed up beside Jewel.

Malachi ran beside the wagon as it rolled away from the homestead and along the creek. A killdeer ran along the other edge on its long toothpick-thin legs. A lone cottonwood stood beside the creek and spread its huge branches out wide over the flat land. Jewel turned at that point out into the prairie and away from the creek.

Sadie noticed the gunbelt that Jewel had strapped around her wide hips. The wide leather holster hid a patch on the side of her dress. Sadie knew the .44 would be too heavy for most women, but Jewel's large, strong hands could handle it easily.

Coyotes yapped, and Malachi pricked his ears but didn't bark.

"That was sure nice of Carl White to follow us home last night," said Jewel. "And he checked all four of the wheels to make double-sure the nuts were on tight." She flashed her pretty smile at Sadie. "He promised to come over for supper before you have to go home."

"I'm glad." Sadie had watched him ride away on

his big white stallion and she'd sighed. It had been fun to listen to him tell about himself as he'd ridden along beside them. He had given Jewel a chance to talk, and that made Sadie like him even better.

"York tells me he wants a first name," said Jewel. "Did you come up with any?"

Sadie watched a red-winged blackbird land on a fence post. "No."

"How about Eli? That was my man's name. Eli Comstock. A good, strong name. What do you think?"

"It doesn't matter to me."

Jewel looked closely at Sadie. "You got something against York?"

The wagon creaked and the harness rattled. "Sometimes he makes me mad."

"You don't say."

"He's too bossy."

"I never noticed. He sure does love your momma."

Sadie rolled her eyes. In all the years Pa and Momma had been together, Sadie had never once seen him kiss or hug her. York didn't care who was around when he hugged and kissed Momma. It was embarrassing. "He yelled at Web and Helen because Bossie got away."

"Yelled? That don't sound like York. Scolded, maybe?"

Sadie shrugged. "I don't think it was their fault."

"You don't?"

"No. I think that orphan boy turned Bossie loose. And if I see him again I'll find out!"

"Speakin' of orphan . . . Look." Jewel motioned up ahead.

"That's him!"

"If that don't beat all. Let's invite him along to pick up chips. It must get mighty lonely for him."

"He deserves it."

"He's just a mite of a boy."

"He's as big as me!"

"You're just a mite of a girl."

Sadie wrinkled her nose. That was true. She wanted to grow tall more than anything, but Momma said it wasn't likely to happen.

"What d' you say, Sadie girl? Shall we ask the boy along?"

Sadie thought of all the things she could say and do to him. "Might as well. His name's Bob."

Jewel slapped the reins on Annie and Ernie to make them go faster so she could catch up to Bob. "Bob. You, boy!" shouted Jewel.

Bob looked back, a frightened look on his small dirty face. He glanced at Sadie, and his face turned fire-red. He looked quickly away from her to Jewel.

"Want to go with us today? You could help get buffalo chips and I'd feed you a good meal. Fried chicken. Biscuits."

Sadie wanted to jump off the wagon and punch the orphan right in his nose, but she sat still and waited.

Finally he nodded. "I'll go with you."

Malachi sniffed at Bob's leg, then licked his hand. Bob patted the dog's head, then ran to the wagon and climbed in the back beside the two baskets.

Jewel talked all the way to the spot where she stopped the wagon. "Now we get to work." She climbed down and lifted the two baskets out of the back. She gave one to Sadie, and she kept one. "Bob, you and Sadie work together."

Sadie grinned. Now was her chance.

"How long have you lived on Cottonwood Creek, Bob?" asked Jewel.

"Not long."

"I hear you paid a visit to the bachelors in the dugout."

Bob hung his head. "I'll pay 'em back as soon as I can."

"They'd probably given you food if you'd asked. Stealin' is a sin. You know that. Everybody knows that."

"I know," mumbled Bob. He hiked up his baggy pants that looked about three sizes too big for him. His bare feet were small and dirty.

"Let's get to work. I thank you both for helping me out. It takes a lot of fuel to keep me warm in the winter. I could buy coal if I had the cash money or something to trade. But I don't have neither, so that's that." She balanced the basket on her hip near her gunbelt. The handle of a .44 stuck out from the holster. "Come, Malachi. Let's go to work." She turned back to Bob and Sadie. "Keep your eye peeled for snakes."

Sadie nodded as she took one handle and Bob the other. She tugged hard to make Bob go the way she wanted. She wanted Bob far enough away from Jewel that she could talk to him however she wanted without Jewel saying anything.

One after another she threw buffalo chips into the basket. For some reason she couldn't bring herself to sock Bob in the eye.

"You're mad at me, aren't you?" asked Bob.

Sadie scowled at him. "Why can't you talk right?"

Bob poked out his chin. "I talk English. You talk American."

"Are you from England?"

"Ma and Pa were."

Sadie saw tears fill Bob's eyes and slowly slip down his dirty cheeks. Sadie frowned. She wanted to hug him close the way she did with Web or Helen when they cried. The thought made her angry at him all over again. "You're such a sissy!"

Bob turned quickly away and knuckled away the tears.

Sadie bit her lip and thought about apologizing. Instead she snapped at his back, "You stole my rabbit."

"I was hungry. I'll pay you back."

"You untied Bossie and took her and Babe away from our house. Didn't you?" Sadie stood beside the basket and waited. She saw Bob's narrow shoulders tense.

Bob whipped around, and sparks shot from his blue eyes. "Yes, I did! But I wasn't stealing."

"No . . . You were rustling cattle!"

"I was not!"

"Rustlers get hung, you know!"

Bob rubbed his dirty neck and swallowed hard. "Will I get hung?"

Sadie flung three chips in the basket before she answered, "I suppose you won't since you're just a mite of a boy."

"I'm as big as you are!"

"Do you know how much trouble you caused by taking Bossie and Babe? York yelled at Web and Helen. You remember Helen? She was with me when we first saw you."

Bob hung his head. "I didn't think about anybody but myself. I wanted the cow so I'd have milk."

"If we wouldn't have found her, then we wouldn't have had milk!"

"I didn't think about that either."

He looked so upset that Sadie didn't have the heart to scold him further. "Let's get to work or we'll never get the wagon full."

By the time the wagon was full late that afternoon Sadie's back ached, and she was sure Jewel's and Bob's did too. Not even Jewel talked as she drove them back to her place. Malachi rode in the wagon beside Bob on the pile of chips. Twice Sadie's eyes closed and her head bobbed, then she jerked awake and forced her eyes wide.

"Drop me off here," said Bob when they reached the huge cottonwood.

Jewel stopped the team and looked back at Bob. "You can come eat supper with us if you have a mind to."

Bob hesitated, but shook his head. He patted Malachi, said good-bye, and jumped from the wagon and ran to the creek.

"He's from England," said Sadie as Jewel slapped the reins against Ernie and Annie.

"That's why he talks funny."

"That's why." Sadie sighed. "I guess I do feel sorry for him."

"I reckon I do too. Poor little mite. He probably made himself a dugout and lives all by his lonesome."

Sadie looked down at her dirty hands to hide the tears that popped in her eyes.

At Jewel's Sadie helped unharness the team. They left the wagon beside the barn where Jewel said they'd unload the chips in the morning. Sadie turned Ernie into the corral, but led Annie inside the cool barn to milk her.

Later just as they finished supper Sadie said, "Oh, no! I forgot to bring in my dress."

"Run out and get it while I clear the table." Jewel rubbed her hands down her clean apron and sighed heavily. "Right after supper we hit the hay. I'm so tired I can't see straight."

Sadie ran to the spot where she'd spread out her dress. The sun had set, but it was still light out. Wind whipped her braids against her neck and her dirty skirts against her tired legs. Ernie whinnied.

With a frown Sadie looked all around the area. She ran back and forth and looked harder. "Oh my! Oh!" Her stomach tightened, and a chill ran down her spine.

Was she so tired that she couldn't see straight?

She looked all the way down to the edge of the creek, up and down the sides of the creek, and right up to Jewel's door.

The dress was gone.

8

The Cornhusk Doll

Her heart hammering loud enough to scare the crickets, Sadie ran to the house and burst through the door.

Jewel spun around from the dishpan, water dripping from her large hands.

"Jewel, my dress is gone!"

"Gone?"

Malachi whined up at Jewel.

She patted his great head. "It's all right, boy."

Sadie twisted her hands in her skirt. A bright red spot dotted each cheek. "It's not all right. I need that dress!"

Jewel grabbed the dishtowel. "Don't get your tail tied in a knot, Sadie girl. It's got to be there somewhere. Maybe a gust of wind blew it away."

Sadie's thin chest rose and fell. "I looked all over, Jewel. It's not anywhere!"

Malachi ran to the door and looked back at Jewel.

She rubbed her hands dry, dropped the towel onto the table, and strode outdoors. The chickens were already roosting for the night, but it was light enough to see. She rested her leather-hard hands on her waist and looked around.

Barely breathing, Sadie waited at Jewel's side.

"It's got to be here someplace." Jewel strode around the yard with long steps, her big black hightop shoes making large puffs of dust.

Sadie ran to keep up with her, her small bare feet making little puffs of dust. "I still don't see it, Jewel. Do you see it?"

"Calm down, Sadie girl."

Sadie took a deep breath, but still her nerves leaped around inside her like the frogs in the creek.

Finally Jewel stopped and shook her head. "I'll be switched. I'll be switched, Sadie girl." She patted Malachi's head. "I'll be switched, Malachi. Where could that dress have got to?"

Sadie felt a flood of tears gathering inside her, filling her, ready to spill out if she said a word. Her body ached from holding herself so rigid. Slowly, slowly she felt the tears melt away inside her, and she wondered if her whole insides were soaked with them.

Jewel rested a hand lightly on Sadie's shoulder. "Sadie, God works miracles. Let's ask Him to help us find your dress in the morning when we look again."

A band tightened around Sadie's heart. She really couldn't have God noticing her, but she did need her dress back, so she nodded.

Jewel lifted her head, and her hook of a nose looked bigger than usual. "Heavenly Father, we love You and thank You that You always take care of us. Help us find Sadie's dress. In the meantime don't let it get ripped or anything."

Sadie cringed as the picture of her torn good dress flashed across her mind. She was so upset she didn't hear the rest of Jewel's prayer.

Jewel tugged on Sadie's arm. "Let's get inside to bed, and in the morning we'll look again."

With her head down Sadie walked to the house. In silence she changed into her nightclothes and crawled under the cover on the pallet Jewel had made her on the floor.

The next morning she pulled on her dirty dress while Jewel still snored in her bed with Malachi on the floor beside her and ran outdoors, the milk pail swinging in her hand. She looked up to see great dark clouds rolling across the sky. Chilly wind whipped against her bare legs below her skirt.

She stopped short beside the wagon. The buffalo chips lay in a big pile just where Jewel wanted them. "Who did that?" She walked around the edge of the pile, shaking her head. Wind blew her tangled hair into her eyes, and she pushed it back. "Who did that?"

Had the bachelors stopped in to do a good turn for Jewel? Wouldn't they have told her? Wouldn't Malachi have barked a warning that someone was there?

A movement at the side of the barn caught her attention. She stiffened. "Who's there?" she called, then louder, "Who's there?"

Annie bawled at the gate.

Sadie wanted to run around the barn and look to see if someone was there, but she couldn't muster up the courage. She tried to swallow, but her throat was too dry.

Suddenly Bob burst across the yard and dashed down along the creek away from the homestead.

Sadie pressed her fingers to her lips. Had Bob unloaded the chips all by himself?

Annie bawled again, and Sadie ran to let her into the barn. Sadie picked up the milk stool that always rested in the same corner beside the pitchfork, then stopped. "That's strange," she whispered.

A pile of straw was spread against the wall, and it hadn't been there last night. Sadie set down the stool and the pail and walked to the straw. The hard-packed dirt floor was cool against her bare feet. Light from the door barely lit the back of the barn. Sadie squatted down by the straw. A cornhusk doll lay almost out of sight in the straw.

"A doll," she whispered through dry lips. She looked quickly around. Someone had slept in the barn. Someone had left a cornhusk doll. Did Bob know who it was?

Sadie pushed the straw over, and her hand touched something softer than straw. She hesitated, then picked it up, and tumbled backward in shock.

"My dress!"

She held it to her as she scrambled to her feet. It was folded neatly. Slowly she unfolded it to find it was still clean. "My dress."

With her eyes closed she pressed it against her face. God had helped her find her dress. He had kept it safe.

But who had hidden it in the barn? Why would anyone want her everyday dress? It was faded and had three patches on it. Nobody could want it. She only wanted it because she needed it.

Annie bawled and looked at her with her big cow eyes.

"I'm comin', Annie." Sadie folded the dress and laid it on the straw with the cornhusk doll on top of it. She picked up the stool and pail and sat at Annie's side and squeezed warm, foaming milk into the pail.

She set the bucket carefully on the barn floor, then

turned Annie back into the corral. She pulled off her dirty dress and slipped on her clean wrinkled one, struggled with the buttons in the back as usual, then tied the sash. She rubbed her hand down it and smiled. "My dress."

She flung her dirty dress over her shoulder, held the doll in one hand and the milk pail in the other, and walked to the dugout.

Jewel flung the door wide and cried, "You're a regular early bird, Sadie girl. And you got the milkin' done." She stared at Sadie's dress. "I'll be switched!"

"My dress." Sadie grinned as she set the pail on the table and rubbed her skirt.

"Thank You, dear God, for answerin'!"

Sadie draped her dirty dress over a chair. "It was folded in the barn, and this was there too." She held out the cornhusk doll.

Jewel took the doll in her hands and turned it over and over. "I'll be switched."

"And all the chips are unloaded in a neat pile right where you wanted them."

Jewel slapped her hand to her forehead. "I'll be double switched! One of them bachelors might've unloaded my chips and maybe folded your dress and put it in the barn in case it rained, but they neither one would carry around a cornhusk doll. Unless it was a gift for you."

Sadie touched the rough cob of a face. She'd had many dolls just like this one, but it'd been a long time ago. The doll she had now was a rag doll that she'd sewed out of scraps. Being a big girl of twelve she couldn't play with it, but she sometimes liked to look at it and think about having a real baby someday to dress and feed and take care of. "Do you think Carl White maybe brought it to me early this mornin'?"

Jewel shrugged. "It don't seem likely, but what other answer do we have?"

Thunder crashed, and Sadie jumped.

Jewel grabbed her hat and pushed it on. "Come on, Malachi. We got chickens to feed and water to bring in before rain comes. It looks like pickin' up chips is out until after the rain passes."

Later rain lashed at the door and window of the dugout and seeped through the thick sod wall beside them. Back away from the front wall it was snug and warm and dry. It would take a lot of water to seep down into the room. Jewel had whitewashed the ceiling and walls, so it was light enough to see with the lamp lit.

Lightning zigzagged across the sky, and thunder cracked. Sadie sat at the table with Jewel and watched the rain streak the window. "I wonder if Bob found a dry place out of the storm."

"I hope so. I'd hate to think he'd get struck with lightning."

Sadie hadn't thought of that. She shivered. "I saw him this morning." She told Jewel about it.

Jewel absently rubbed Malachi's ears. "I wonder if he unloaded the wagon."

"Me too." Sadie picked up the doll and carefully touched the dry husk. "I sure hate to think of Bob out in this storm. I wish I could find him and bring him here."

"You took quite a shine to that boy, didn't you?"

She hated to admit it, but she had. "There's such sadness in his eyes sometimes that it almost makes me cry."

Jewel nodded. "I've seen it myself. Poor little mite."

Sadie wanted to get up and pace, but the area was too small. She thought about Momma, York, and the kids in the tiny soddy, and she knew they didn't have room to pace either. She looked across the small table at Jewel. "Maybe Bob would go home with me and live with us."

"Maybe he don't want to live with anyone but himself."

That made Sadie sad.

"He's afraid of people. But Malachi and him sure took to each other. It's not like Malachi at all, especially when he first meets someone. It usually takes him a while to make up his mind." Jewel kissed Malachi between the ears. "But you took right to that mite of a boy, didn't you?"

Malachi slapped the hard-packed dirt floor with his rope of a tail.

Thunder rumbled, and the rain let up. Sadie held the doll tighter. Maybe she could try to find Bob after the storm was over. Could she talk him into finding a regular home? Maybe with them?

9

Danger

Just outside Jewel's door Sadie blinked at the suddenly bright sunlight that pushed the last of the storm clouds away. Steam rose from the damp ground. Water dripped from the leaves of the two cottonwoods, but they too soon dried from the intense heat of the sun.

"You go out and look for Bob, but be back before noon so we can go pick up chips," Jewel had said when Sadie had asked if she could go. "But don't go any further than the lone cottonwood where the flat land starts."

Sadie ran along the edge of the creek. The sand on top was dry, but her toes curled into damp sand underneath as she ran. Wind tugged at her bonnet, and she pushed it off her head to let it dangle down between her sharp shoulder blades. Her dark braids danced on her shoulders. Birds sang at the top of their lungs. A frog splashed into the creek, and another one croaked.

Suddenly Sadie stopped. Maybe she should've

looked in the barn first for the person who had slept there. She glanced back, but a small hill blocked her view and only the top of the barn was in sight. Maybe Bob would know. She hesitated, then shrugged. "I'll look when I get back."

In the distance she heard a loud bellow of a bull and she trembled, glad a fence separated Jewel's cattle from her. She'd seen the huge black bull when it had pushed against the corral fence. At first she'd thought it was a buffalo, but Jewel had assured her it wasn't.

Up ahead she saw Bob standing at the edge of the water, fishing with a crude fishing pole. Sadie sighed in relief. She'd thought she'd find him soaked to the skin, shivering and frightened, or even flat-out on the ground, fried dead from a lightning strike.

"Bob!" she called and waved.

He jerked and dropped the pole. He turned his head and saw her, then leaped away down the creek away from her. His baggy clothes flapped as he ran.

She frowned. Why was he afraid of her again? Had he stolen something else? "Wait, Bob! Come back!" She flew after him, running with all of her might.

Sweat broke out on her face, but the wind dried it. Inside she was screaming at Bob for running away from her, but she kept all the words inside to conserve energy for running.

He looked over his shoulder, his face white and for once clean. He stumbled slightly and lost stride.

She closed the distance between them. She could hear his labored breathing. Sand spit out from under his bare feet.

A few minutes later Sadie sailed through the air and tackled Bob around the legs. They fell, sprawling heavily half in and half out of the shallow creek.

Her chest heaving, Sadie jumped to her feet and

looked down at Bob. Water dripped from the left side of her dress. "What's wrong with you?" she screamed down at him. "I only wanted to talk to you and see if you were all right after the storm!" Her voice rang out over the creek and the prairie and bounced off the hills. "How come you ran away from me?"

Bob's shoulders shook, and Sadie heard a sob.

Impatiently she nudged his side with her toes. "Are you cryin'?"

Bob pushed himself up into a sitting position on the sand and huddled into himself, his face buried against his wet knees. His slight body shook, and great sobs tore from him.

Sadie's anger turned to concern. Maybe she'd broken every bone in his body. Neither Web nor Riley would cry like this in front of anyone, probably not even if they were alone, no matter how badly they were hurt. She dropped beside him. "Did I hurt you? What's wrong?"

He sobbed harder.

Sadie shook his bony shoulder. "Stop that! You're scaring me!"

His body shook so much, it looked like his clothes were whipping in the wind the way they did on a clothesline.

Sadie rubbed an unsteady hand over her face. "Bob? Don't cry. I didn't mean to hurt you."

A bull bellowed again, this time closer. A chill ran over Sadie, and she looked quickly around. The lone cottonwood stood some distance away, and the flat land stretched out with only Jewel's wagon tracks to break its monotony. Sadie bit her lip. Just how far away was Jewel's fence line?

Bob lifted his head slightly. "The bull," he whispered.

Sadie saw his tear-streaked face, and for a minute he reminded her of Helen. She frowned at the strange thought. "We don't have to worry about the bull. It's fenced in."

"The . . . the fence is down."

"What?" Sadie shrieked. "And Jewel's cattle got out and you didn't come tell her?" Her dark eyes flashed, and she doubled her fists at her sides.

"I . . . I was afraid to talk to her."

Sadie couldn't believe her ears. "Why?"

Bob looked down at the clump of grass beside him. "I . . . just was."

Sadie flung out her arms and strode two steps away and two steps back. "We've got to tell her and get the cattle back in and the fence fixed right away."

Bob sniffed and rubbed his eyes.

Just then Sadie heard a snort behind her. She turned, and her eyes widened in shock. Jewel's huge black bull stood some distance away with his great head down, pawing the ground with one hoof. Sand and bits of grass flew up from its hoof and hit against its shaggy hide. Its powerful sharp, curved horns glistened in the sunlight.

Another time and another bull flashed across her mind. As if it had happened minutes ago instead of when she was ten she saw Pa's friend, Mr. Jacobs, ride his horse into the pasture where he kept his cattle. With a mighty roar his bull ran away from the cows toward Mr. Jacobs. Pa yelled for Mr. Jacobs to get out of there, but he'd yelled back that the bull was just noise and wouldn't hurt a flea. Suddenly the bull charged the horse, goring its flank. Squealing in agony, the horse bucked and Mr. Jacobs flew through the air and landed with a thud on the ground. The bull charged him and tossed him up into the air, then tossed him again. Blood spurted everywhere. Pa grabbed his rifle and shot the bull, but Mr. Jacobs was dead, gored to death by the bull that wouldn't hurt a flea.

Jewel's bull snorted again.

Sadie shuddered.

Bob inched closer to her and slipped his hand in hers. She jerked and stared at Bob in surprise. She saw the fear on his face and in his eyes. Her hand closed over his, and it felt like Helen's hand.

Frantically Sadie looked around for a way to escape. Silently she cried out for God to help her.

If they ran into the creek, the bull would follow. And it was too far back to Jewel's to outrun the bull. Sadie saw the splendid cottonwood standing some distance away with wide, solid branches low enough to climb. Her heart jumped.

"We gotta run to the tree and climb it before the bull charges," whispered Sadie, barely able to get the words past the hard lump in her throat.

"Oh, Sadie."

"When I say run, let's go." Wind flapped her skirts and pushed against her body. She was glad the wind would be against their backs, helping them run.

The bull snorted louder, pawed one more time, then charged right at them with its head down.

"Run!" Sadie tugged on Bob's hand, but he slipped and fell. She looked up and could almost feel the great curved horns pierce her body and see her blood spurt all over.

The ground shook as the bull ran closer.

Sadie hauled Bob to his feet. Tensely she waited. The bull thundered closer still, its mighty horns threatening. When it was too close to change directions to gore them, Sadie jumped aside, hauling Bob with her.

She could smell the bull's damp hide and feel the heat from its great body.

She jerked Bob's hand, and they raced for the giant cottonwood. Her legs seemed to weigh more than Jewel's wagon axle. Her feet seemed to cling to the ground. Against her will she glanced back to see the bull hesitate in the middle of the creek, size them up, then thunder after them. Water splashed up and sparkled in the sun.

Bob stumbled, but Sadie tightened her grip and he caught his balance and ran harder. She could feel the bull's hot breath on her legs.

She reached the tree and caught at the lowest rough limb, swung her leg over, and scrambled up through the rough branches and dancing leaves. Finally she glanced down. Her heart stopped. Bob's pant leg had caught on a twig, and he couldn't climb any higher than the first branch.

The bull crashed into the tree, and Bob screamed and looked as if he'd fall right down onto the bull's horns. The bull fell back, stunned for a minute, then shook its great head.

"Help me, Sadie!" Bob cried.

She hesitated, her heart pounding.

"Sadie!"

Trembling, she scrambled down. The bull's breath was hot against her ankles. She clamped her lips against the scream that threatened to escape. Her hand shook as she reached out to tug the pant leg loose. She tugged twice, then again, and it pulled free. The bull snorted and shook its head. Bob climbed up, and Sadie followed. The bull roared up at them. It tore loose a twig, flung it to the ground, and trampled it.

Bob burst into tears and pushed his face against the rough branch.

Sadie struggled against her tears. She glared at Bob. "Don't be such a sissy!" she cried.

Bob sniffed. "I'm not a sissy!"

"You are too. You're acting just like Helen."

"So what?" snapped Bob. He leaned against the tree trunk and clung to his branch. "I can act like a girl if I want. I *am* a girl!"

Sadie sagged weakly against her branch and stared at him. "A girl?"

"And I want my doll. Where is she?"

"Your doll?"

"I left her in the barn."

"The cornhusk doll?"

"Amanda. Ma made her for me."

"Amanda?" Sadie's head spun. For a moment she forgot about the bull. "You are a girl and that doll is yours?"

Bob lifted his head, and suddenly Sadie could see by the fine bones of his face that he was a girl.

"My name is Mary Elizabeth Ferguson."

"Not Bob?"

"Bob was my pa."

Sadie shook her head. "But why pretend to be a boy?"

Mary was quiet a long time. The bull snorted below. "It was safer to be a boy."

"Are you really an orphan?"

"Yes."

Sadie clicked her tongue. "I can't believe it."

"It's the truth!"

"I mean I can't believe you're a girl. I can't believe I didn't know you were a girl. You kept acting like one. You even look like one. Even with that haircut."

Mary touched her hair. "I cut it myself with a knife."

"I can cut it to look better."

"You can?"

Sadie nodded, then frowned. "We'd better figure out a way out of here before we talk about cuttin' your hair."

She watched the bull walk away from the tree and stop in the tall grass to graze. It lifted its head and looked right at her, and she cringed. She knew if they even tried to get down, the bull would charge. She shuddered. She didn't want to be gored. With a shiver she pushed the terrible thought aside.

She rubbed her sleeve, then shot a look at Mary. "You took my dress, didn't you?"

Mary hung her head. "I saw it there, and I knew it would fit me." She scratched the side of her small nose. "It's been so long since I wore a dress. I wanted to try it on and then I was going to give it back." She sniffled and knuckled a tear from her eye. "I tried it on and I wanted it so bad I couldn't give it back. I'm . . . sorry."

She looked sorry. Sadie sighed. "I forgive you."

"You do? Thank you." Mary smiled, and for a minute the terrible sadness left her eyes. "Can we be friends, do you think?"

Sadie nodded. "Maybe you could come live with us."

Mary shook her head. "Your ma and pa wouldn't want me."

"Sure they would." But would they? They didn't have much room.

Mary glanced down at the bull and sighed. "Maybe we won't ever find out. We might be up here forever."

Sadie gripped the branch tighter and curled her toes into the one she stood on. "Don't worry, Mary. God will help us. He is always with us." The words shocked

Sadie to her very depth. Had she really said that? Did she believe it?

In the distance Sadie heard the sound of a creaking wagon and Jewel's loud shout.

Sadie waved wildly with her free arm. "We're up here, Jewel! Up in the cottonwood. Be careful of your bull!"

Jewel waved back. As she drew closer, Sadie saw she carried a long bullwhip that Sadie had seen hanging in her barn. Jewel cracked the whip and stung the bull's nose. It roared and pawed the ground. She cracked the whip again. The bull turned away from it.

Over and over the crack of the whip echoed over the prairie until finally the bull ran back toward Jewel's place. Sadie breathed a sigh of relief.

Jewel drove the wagon as close to the tree as she could. "I had a feelin' deep in my heart that you kids needed help."

"We did," said Mary.

"Thanks, Jewel," said Sadie. She started to tell God thank you too, but she hesitated.

She scrambled down the tree and ran to the wagon. "Bob's a girl, Jewel. His name's Mary Elizabeth Ferguson."

Jewel's mouth dropped open, and she stared at Mary as she climbed up in the wagon beside Sadie. "I'll be switched," Jewel finally said.

"Me too," said Sadie with a laugh.

"When we get back to my place I want to hear your story, Mary Elizabeth Ferguson," said Jewel.

Mary looked down at her bare feet.

"We want to hear it all," said Sadie.

10

The Orphan's Story

Sadie studied Mary thoughtfully as they helped stretch the barbed wire so Jewel could nail in the staples to hold it to the new fence post. It had taken quite a while to get the cattle back inside the pasture, but with Jewel's bullwhip and loud voice they'd done it.

Jewel wiped the sweat from the band of her hat, and off her forehead, rammed her hat back on, and stuffed her handkerchief under her gunbelt. "Let's take a breather before we go after buffalo chips, girls." Jewel threw back her head and laughed. "Girls! I still can't get over you bein' a girl, Mary Ferguson."

Mary flushed and twisted her toe in the sand. "I hope you're not mad at me for living in your barn."

"Not at all!" Jewel clamped a leather-hard hand on Sadie's shoulder. "You've been mighty quiet, Sadie girl. What's goin' on in that head of yours?"

Sadie glanced up at Jewel, then over at Mary. "We still haven't heard her story."

"You're right about that. But first things had to come first. The cattle and the fence wouldn't wait." She scratched Malachi between the ears. "What say we go sit in the shade of the cottonwood you girls perched in a while ago and listen to a story?"

Sadie climbed in the wagon and sat on the seat between Jewel and Mary. No one spoke as Jewel drove away from the fence and around a hill to the huge cottonwood.

A meadowlark warbled from a swaying piece of timothy grass. A flock of ducks flew across the wide blue sky that stretched forever down, down to the green rolling hills.

A few minutes later Sadie sat cross-legged under the cottonwood with Jewel leaning against the rough trunk and Mary sitting with a hand on Malachi's head. "Don't leave anything out, Mary," said Sadie.

Mary trembled, and Malachi licked her cheek. "I don't know where to start."

"With your family," said Jewel.

Mary flicked a tear from her long lashes. "I had three brothers, James, Edward, and Henry, and one sister, Ruth." Her voice broke and she swallowed hard. "We started out with Ma and Pa from Iowa on a wagon train. Pa wanted to come to Nebraska for his own property and to start over. From the time he'd arrived from England he'd worked for the same farmer, and he'd never had a place of his own. He said it wasn't right for a man not to have land. He said a man should have land to pass to his sons. I guess his daughters didn't count." She picked at the knee of her baggy pants. "So we came west. But something terrible happened."

Sadie leaned forward and locked her fingers together.

"People started getting sick, really sick. Some of our friends died. Ruth died, and I cried so hard I couldn't eat for days."

"I know how that is," whispered Jewel, blinking away tears.

Mary sucked in her breath, but a sob escaped. "James and Henry got real sick, then Edward, then Pa, and last Ma."

Sadie couldn't look at Mary any longer or she knew she'd start to cry. She'd felt terrible when Pa had died in the blizzard, but she'd still had Momma and the kids.

Mary twisted a ragged piece of dark hair around her finger. "They died, and I had to be put with another family on the train. Nobody wanted me, but they couldn't just leave me all alone where no one lived. So Mr. and Mrs. Swanson took me with them. They had a daughter my age. Niva." Mary's blue eyes flashed with sudden anger. "She was spoiled and naughty and made a lot of trouble for me. I didn't like her at all."

"I wouldn't either," said Sadie.

"One night when what was left of the wagon train stopped for the night, Niva let the horses go and said I did it. It made everyone mad at me. I tried to tell them, but they wouldn't listen." Mary's voice rose and she stopped, took a deep breath, and continued in her normal voice. "When they finally got the horses back, everybody voted that I be kicked out of the train. Mr. Swanson rode to the nearest town to find a home for what he called a troublemaking orphan. That was me." Mary tapped her chest with a dirty finger. "He told them I was strong and a hard worker. They didn't know he was lying. Mr. and Mrs. Oscar said they needed help on their farm, and they didn't have any kids, so they said they'd take me. Once they'd had a boy, but he'd died when he was fourteen. They were mad when they saw I was small for my age and not very strong.

"I worked hard for them, but they got mad when I couldn't do a lot. They beat me and wouldn't let me go to town ever."

Jewel slapped her knee. "I'd give them a piece of my mind if I had a chance! Makes me mad just to hear you tell it."

Mary smiled weakly at Jewel. "I decided I'd run away, but it was winter and I had to wait for spring. I found some clothes that had belonged to their boy and I took them. I cut off my hair and I took only the corn-husk doll, Amanda, that Ma had made me. The clothes were too big, but I wore them anyway. The cap made me look different, and I knew even Mr. and Mrs. Oscar wouldn't recognize me."

Sadie couldn't imagine what Mary looked like with long hair and a dress.

Malachi leaned his head on Mary's lap.

"One day when they were going to town I hid under a tarp they had in the back of their wagon. It was hot and smelly, and I thought for sure they'd notice me, but they didn't. As soon as they got to town and went inside the store, I jumped out and walked away."

"Good for you," said Sadie.

"Were you afraid?" asked Jewel.

Mary nodded with a faraway look in her eye. "I walked around town for a while and then I saw another wagon all loaded, so I hid in it. It brought me all the way to Jake's Crossing. The man never knew I was in his wagon. It was hard to walk after being cramped for so long." Mary rubbed her back as if it hurt just thinking about it.

"I hung around town a while, but it was hard to find food. I slept in the livery until they caught me and kicked me out. I tried to get a job, but I was too small."

"One day Carl White and Sven Johnson were in town, and I heard them talking about Cottonwood Creek and how they loved to live there. They made it sound so good, I decided I'd like to live there, even if I had to live all by myself. I thought I could make a dugout like I'd heard the bachelors lived in." Mary sighed loud and long. "But I couldn't. I found a sod barn and made friends with a big dog, and I slept in the barn at night and got out before daylight."

Jewel chuckled. "I can understand now why Malachi greeted you as a friend."

"He didn't know if he should trust me at first." Mary patted his back. "But I talked to him, and before long he started liking me."

"I'm surprised Jewel didn't catch you sleepin' in the barn," said Sadie.

"She almost did a few times, but I always managed to sneak out before she saw me." Mary looked sheepishly at Jewel. "I sometimes went in your dugout and ate a biscuit or slept on your bed when I knew you'd be gone for the day."

"I'll be switched!"

"I'm gonna see if Momma and York will let Mary live with us," said Sadie. Just then a strange feeling fluttered inside her, and she realized that she was homesick.

She gazed across the prairie in the direction of her home. She wasn't like Mary. She had a family.

Oh, how she longed to see them! She'd hug them all, even Opal and even York.

But would they be glad to see her? Would they want her to hug them? Helen would, but the others probably were glad she was gone. They probably didn't miss her at all.

A great sadness filled her, and she wanted to cover her face and bawl at the top of her lungs.

11
The Haircut

Slowly Sadie picked up another buffalo chip. She dragged the almost-full burlap bag along beside her. Jewel and Mary had the baskets. The late-afternoon sun burned against her back. Wind gusted and almost blew her off her feet, but it didn't cool her.

She looked at Mary, so far away that she was a big black dot on the prairie, and at Jewel with Malachi in the opposite direction, other black dots. Jewel had left the team and wagon in the center, and each of them had walked out from it.

"It'll be quicker if we each work our own space, then bring the full containers back to the wagon," Jewel had said, studying the sky. "We want to get done and back home before we get some weather."

Sighing, Sadie looked toward her home. If she were home right now she'd be helping with supper.

What were they eating tonight? Probably the deer Levi had brought. Momma made the best venison roast with onions and carrots and potatoes. But Sadie knew they wouldn't have onions and carrots and potatoes until the garden came in. So Momma would make a roast, and with the drippings make a thick gravy to eat over wide egg noodles that had dried for almost three hours on a cloth spread over the table. Opal had probably baked bread today, and they'd have thick slices of fresh bread spread with butter.

Sadie bit her lower lip as she pushed another buffalo chip into the sack. "If I were home I would've made the noodles." She could see herself mixing together flour and salt with a pinch of baking powder. She'd make a hole in the mixture and add three beat-up eggs with a little milk and stir the stiff yellow mixture together. If it wasn't stiff enough she'd add more flour, then drop it on the flour-covered cloth on the table, sprinkle more flour on it, and roll it thin with Momma's heavy wooden rolling pin, but not so thin that it cracked. She'd cut the dough into long strips about an inch wide. When they dried on one side, she'd very carefully turn them over to dry on the other side. When the roast was done, Momma would pour off the broth into a kettle. While she made gravy with it, Sadie would boil salted water in another kettle, then carefully drop each noodle into the water, boil them about three minutes, drain them and pour them into a white ironstone bowl, and set them on the table where everyone would be hungrily waiting for supper.

A tear slipped down Sadie's cheek, leaving a clean trail. The wind dried it before it slid off her chin.

A dust devil swirled across the flat land, and another one followed it. Sand gritted between Sadie's teeth, and her lips felt caked with dirt. She scratched an itch on her leg. From the bottom of her skirts up, her leg looked almost white next to the brown of her legs from the bottom of her skirts down to her feet.

"Oh, no!" She touched her cheek. She'd left her bonnet off all day long. Her face was probably as brown as her feet and legs. Momma had told her over and over to wear her bonnet while she worked in the sun.

"I don't want you looking like a wild Indian, Sadie," Momma had said many times.

Sadie had wanted to say that she liked the color of wild Indians, but she knew she dare not talk back to Momma, no matter how badly she wanted to.

Malachi barked a warning, and Sadie stiffened. She shielded her eyes against the sun with her hand and looked toward Malachi. What did he see? Jewel had said, "If Malachi barks his warning bark, you girls hightail it right for the wagon."

Sadie hoisted the sack on her back and ran as fast as she could. The sack flopped awkwardly, making it hard to run. Maybe she should drop the sack. She shook her head and ran harder, both hands gripping the sack at her shoulder.

Just as she reached the wagon Mary screamed. Sadie's heart jerked. She pushed the sack into the wagon and looked for Mary.

A man on a roan was riding hard right at Mary. A shiver ran down Sadie's back. She heard Jewel shout as she ran toward Mary, but Sadie couldn't understand what she said because of Malachi's barking and the strong wind.

Thoughts of what to do buzzed around inside Sadie's head. Finally she scrambled into the wagon and grabbed the reins. They filled her hands. She whipped the reins against Annie and Ernie. Ernie squealed with surprise, and Annie threw up her head and shook it.

"Get up!" shouted Sadie, slapping the reins against them again. "Get up! Annie! Ernie!"

The wagon lurched forward, almost sending Sadie flying out. She braced her bare feet on the floor and held the reins with both hands. She bounced around on the seat as the team ran faster. She saw the man scoop Mary up into the saddle.

"Mary!" screamed Sadie. "Put her down! Mary!"

The man turned his roan toward Sadie. She could see the surprised look on his face. His eyes were as blue as Mary's and his skin a smooth bronze. Blond hair hung from under his wide-brimmed brown hat. He was one of the fine young men that Opal was always looking for.

Sadie saw Mary bite his arm. He yelled and jerked away, and Mary jumped to the ground and raced for the wagon.

Sadie pulled back on the reins. "Whoa!"

The team stopped, and Mary scrambled in and jumped behind Sadie.

The man pulled his pistol and aimed it right at Sadie. Fear stung her skin. "Get out of that wagon, you two rapscallions!" he said in a Swedish accent.

"Don't shoot!" shouted Jewel.

"Don't shoot," whispered Sadie.

The man turned his head and spotted Jewel. He pushed his pistol back in the holster, and Sadie could breathe again. The roan pranced nervously, and the man pulled him up short. "What is going on here? Did these children steal your wagon, Jewel Comstock?"

Gasping for breath, she pulled off her hat and mopped her red face. "They're helpin' me."

The man waved his arm toward Mary. The big sleeve of his gray shirt flapped in the wind. "You let that thievin' orphan help you?"

Jewel nodded.

The man shook his head. "Wait until I tell Carl."

"Come for supper tonight and we'll all talk about it," said Jewel, her breath still coming in gasps.

"I don't know as I want to eat with that thievin' boy, but Carl and me, we like your cooking, so we will come."

"Good," said Jewel with a smile.

The man tipped his hat to Jewel, scowled at Sadie and Mary, nudged his roan and rode away.

"Who was that?" asked Sadie.

"One of the bachelors," whispered Mary.

"Sven Johnson," said Jewel as she weakly helped Malachi into the wagon, then climbed in herself. She smelled sweaty.

"I don't want to see him ever again," said Mary in a weak voice.

Jewel shook her finger at Mary and looked very stern. "You're gonna see him tonight, and you're gonna apologize for stealin' from them."

Sadie patted Mary's arm. "They won't be mad at you when they know your story. So don't be afraid."

The team moved restlessly. Malachi licked Mary's cheek.

"Let's get them chips and get home," said Jewel, motioning toward Mary's basket. "I can't take more excitement today."

Later at Jewel's, while Jewel and Mary did the chores Sadie washed out both her dresses.

She touched her nightdress and hoped no one would come around and see her wearing it in broad daylight. She wrung both dresses out, water running down her arms to drip off her elbows. With the wind blowing as hard as it was, she knew the dresses would dry fast if she had a clothesline, but she didn't. "I could hang 'em on the cottonwood, but they might get ripped on a branch."

With a sigh she looked around for a way to dry them in the wind. "I guess I'll be the clothesline," she said with a grin. She spread one dress on the grass and held up the other by the hem. The wind whipped it out from her and almost jerked it out of her hands. It flapped water back on her, but it felt cool and pleasant against her hot skin. In just a short time both dresses were dry except around the heavy seam at the waist. She carried them inside and hung them over the chairs. If they weren't dry before it was time to change for the bachelors, they'd wear them with wet waist seams.

She heated Jewel's flat iron on the stove, stuck the loaves of bread in the oven that she'd left to rise before they'd gone out for buffalo chips, then carefully ironed away at the wrinkles in the dresses. The hot smell of the iron when it touched the cotton material turned her stomach. When she finished she carefully draped the dresses over Jewel's chairs. The dresses looked clean and pressed, but still faded and old.

"Someday I will have a brand-new dress for good and a brand-new dress for everyday!"

Sadie clapped her hand to her mouth. Had she really said that? How could she be so selfish? She shouldn't want two new dresses if Helen and Opal and Momma had only their old ones.

Sadie lifted her small chin and squared her shoulders. "I wish we all had brand-new dresses for good and brand-new dresses for everyday." She'd never heard of anyone having a brand-new everyday dress. She felt very elegant just saying it. "And I wish Riley and Web and even York had brand-new clothes." She heard Jewel singing outdoors. "And I wish Jewel and Mary would have brand-new clothes."

Sadie grinned. Would she recognize Jewel if she wore women's shoes and a dress that wasn't faded and patched?

What would Mary look like in a dress instead of her boy's clothes?

Mary burst through the door. "I'm done. Are you ready?"

Sadie nodded and held up Jewel's shears. "Sit close to the window so I can see what I'm doin'." It was going to be fun to cut Mary's hair.

Mary giggled and sat down with her back to Sadie. She picked up Amanda and held her tightly. The husk crackled. "It's nice of you to let me wear your dress for tonight."

"That's okay. I can't wear two at the same time." Sadie could hear Pa's voice as if it was yesterday. "Why do you need a new good dress, Sadie? You can't wear two good dresses at the same time."

Mary looked over her shoulder, her fine brows puckered. "What's the matter, Sadie?"

"Nothin'." Sadie took a deep breath and pushed the remembrance of Pa away. She lifted a strand of Mary's hair and saw the copper glints in the brown. Carefully she cut the back even to hang neatly on Mary's thin neck. She trimmed the sides to hang even with Mary's jawline, then parted the top in the center and combed it down. Snip. Snip. She cut two stray pieces to make all the hair even, then stood back and nodded. "It looks good, Mary."

Mary ran to Jewel's looking glass and peered in. She didn't say anything for a long time, but she touched her hair first on one side and then another. She felt the back. "Ma would hate to see my hair so short. It used to hang almost to my waist, and Ma would braid it in two long braids like yours and sometimes she'd tie ribbons on the braids." Mary turned to face Sadie. "I wish I had my long braids back."

"Me too. But your hair will grow, and before you know it it'll be long again." Sadie ducked her head so Mary wouldn't see how bad she felt for her as she swept up the hair on the floor and dropped it in the stove. The smell of burned hair filled the dugout, but soon it was gone and was once again covered by the delicious smell of yeast bread baking in the oven.

Sadie pointed to her dresses. "Mary, you take your choice. Which one do you want to wear?"

Mary studied them both a long time. "It's a hard choice. You pick the one you want and I'll wear the other one."

Sadie chose the most faded one and left the other for Mary. Mary deserved to wear the best dress since it was the first time in a long time that she'd worn a dress. "We better hurry before the bachelors get here. I'd hate to have them see me in my nightdress."

She giggled, and Mary did too.

12

The Bachelors

Jewel stopped in the doorway and stared with her mouth open at Mary. Wind howled outdoors, and the daylight was almost gone. A lamp glowed on the table and another one near the stove.

"Doesn't she look different?" Sadie stood to the side of Mary, feeling as proud as if she'd made her.

Jewel pulled off her hat and slapped her leg. "I'll be switched."

Malachi sniffed Mary, then sniffed her again before he let her touch him.

"I wouldn't know you're the same person. You're a pretty little mite. Yes, you are."

Mary flushed and ducked her head. She did look small and delicate and pretty in Sadie's dress. "Thank you. I was prettier when my hair was long."

Jewel strode to her trunk, lifted the lid, and pulled

out two blue ribbons the very color of Mary's eyes and one of the colors of the flowers in the dress. "I wore these ribbons in my hair a few years back when Eli was still with me. I'll tie them in your hair, and you'll be prettier than a picture." Jewel picked up a wide strand of hair just at the right side of Mary's part and tied a ribbon to it. She did the same on the left side. It pulled the hair back from Mary's face and showed off her high cheekbones and bright blue eyes. The blue ribbons against her copper-brown hair did indeed look pretty.

Mary touched the ribbons gently as she gazed in awe in the looking glass. "I do look pretty." She turned to Jewel. "Thank you, Jewel. I'll take very good care of your ribbons."

"I know you will, honey." Jewel blew her nose and wiped her eyes. "I best get a move on or them boys will catch me in my work clothes. Can't have company for supper and not get cleaned up for 'em."

While Jewel changed, Sadie opened the oven door and heat blasted her face. She lifted out a loaf of bread and set it on the oven door, then thumped it the way Momma had showed her to check to see if it was done. It was golden-brown all over, except for one burned edge. She thumped it again, heard the right sound, then carried it to the table and turned it out of the pan on its side. She did the same to the other two loaves. Three fat loaves of bread sent steam rising in the air. The delicious aroma made Sadie's stomach cramp with hunger.

"Smells good," said Mary, breathing deeply.

"It does," said Sadie. She brushed some of the yellow butter that she'd churned last night onto the top crust, and it turned it to a rich honey-brown.

Jewel stepped from around the sheet that she'd

pulled across her bed for privacy and held her arms out and turned slowly. "How do I look?"

"Beautiful!" cried Mary.

Sadie stared in surprise. Jewel wore a rich green dress and a pair of shoes just like Momma's. A gold heart-shaped brooch was pinned at her throat. Her hair was piled up on her head and looked very elegant. Only her hook nose marred her looks, but Sadie decided she liked Jewel's nose. It was a fine, strong nose for Jewel. "You look grand," said Sadie.

"Thank you, girls. I haven't had a reason to dress like this in a long time. I'm surprised the dress still fits." She touched her wide waist and smoothed down the rich folds of the dress. "It's a bit hot, but I'll survive, I reckon."

Malachi tipped his head and looked up at her and whined.

"It's still me, boy. It sure is." She kissed him between the ears, and he slapped the hard-packed dirt floor with his tail, then settled down in his regular spot beside Jewel's bed.

Jewel tied her apron in place, and it looked even shabbier next to her nice dress. "Your bread looks perfect, Sadie girl. You can bake for me anytime you want."

Sadie smiled. "I've been bakin' bread since I was seven. I would've started sooner, but Opal wouldn't let me take a turn. Finally Momma said all girls had to learn to bake good bread."

"I never learned," said Mary sadly.

"I'll teach you sometime if you want," said Sadie.

Jewel made coffee while the girls fried up potatoes that Jewel had put aside for a special day. Jewel opened a jar of meat that she'd canned last fall and poured it into a heavy black skillet. When the meat and broth were hot, she thickened it with a flour and water paste. She opened a jar of applesauce and poured it in a bowl.

The lamp cast a warm glow over the table as Mary set the plates on. Jewel pulled out her good napkins and set them on the table. The edges were frayed, and all of the napkins had stains that could never be removed.

Malachi lifted his head and barked one short bark. A minute later Sadie heard hoofbeats. She trembled. The supper was suddenly as exciting to her as to Jewel.

Jewel flung wide the door. Wind blew dust in. She shouted out into the night, "Glad you made it, boys. Come on in."

Carl White stepped in first, almost filling the doorway with his size, his white hat in his hand, his dark hair slicked back. Sven Johnson followed, his hat in his hand, his blond curls wild on his head. He looked toothpick-thin next to Carl.

"Howdy," they both said at once.

"Howdy," said Jewel.

Sadie and Mary whispered, "Hello."

"Carl, Sven, this is Sadie and Mary. They're guests for supper too." She patted Malachi's great head. "You go lay down, boy. They're stayin' for supper."

Malachi padded to his spot near Jewel's bed, turned around three times, and laid down with his head on his paws.

"Glad to meet you, girls," said Carl, tipping his head at the girls. "I did meet York's girl the other day, didn't I?"

"Smells good in here," said Sven, sniffing with a look of delight on his thin face.

Carl turned to Jewel. "I hear you had that rascal orphan working for you today."

"Sure did," said Jewel with a chuckle.

Sadie hid a smile and peeked at Mary. She stepped closer to Sadie and didn't smile.

"That boy will steal all your food when you're not looking," said Carl gruffly.

"I should have thrashed him when I had the chance," said Sven.

Sadie felt Mary stiffen.

"Boys, boys, sit down and take a load off your feet. Hang your hats there." She pointed to the pegs next to her hat.

They hung their hats and sat on the only two chairs.

Jewel pulled off her apron and hung it over her old dress on a peg near her bed. "Boys, we'll have a fine supper and then we'll discuss the orphan."

"Suits me," said Carl.

Jewel prayed over the food, and then she offered fried potatoes to the men. They helped themselves as they talked about the terrible wind, the price of beef, how much hay they'd need to winter their cattle, and how much they wanted to claim more ground.

Sadie filled her plate with potatoes, meat and gravy, applesauce with apple chunks still in it, and a thick slice of bread and butter. She sat on the edge of Jewel's bed with Mary and Jewel beside her. She listened as Jewel and the men talked, but she and Mary ate in silence. She didn't care. She was hungry and the food was delicious. She wanted more potatoes, but Sven took the last of them. They ate all three loaves of bread, dunking the slices in the good gravy or the applesauce.

After the meal the men pushed back from the table, crossed their legs, and talked to Jewel while Sadie and Mary washed and dried the dishes. Wind rattled the window. No wind could blow through the thick sod of the front wall or through the hill they were burrowed into.

"We should whitewash our walls like this," said Carl.

"It takes a good long time for the walls to dry enough so you can whitewash them," said Jewel. "You boys will probably be married and have regular homes built by then."

Sadie and Mary hung up their dishtowels and walked back to sit on the bed with Jewel. Sadie's eyes were heavy and she wanted to curl up and go to sleep, but she knew Jewel loved company and loved to talk. Probably the bachelors did too.

Finally Carl leaned forward and said, "Now, we want to talk about the orphan."

"Do you?" Jewel slapped her knee and laughed her great laugh.

The bachelors looked at each other questioningly, then at Jewel. Sadie giggled under her breath. She glanced at Mary, but Mary wasn't even smiling. Her face was pale, and she looked like she was going to burst into tears. Suddenly Sadie didn't feel much like laughing either.

"What's going on here?" asked Sven stiffly. "Is there a joke we do not understand?"

Jewel tugged Mary to her feet. "Boys, meet Mary, your naughty orphan."

"What?" cried Carl, jumping up so quickly his chair almost tipped over.

Malachi growled deep in his throat, and Jewel patted his head.

"A girl?" asked Sven, leaning forward.

"A girl!" cried Carl. "Is this a joke, Jewel Comstock?"

"Not at all. Sit down, please." Jewel waited until Carl sat down again, his eyes hard on Mary.

Sadie locked her icy hands in her lap and suddenly felt wide-awake.

Jewel slipped an arm around Mary. "You have something to say to these boys, Mary."

Mary stepped forward, her chin in the air. "I am sorry I stole your food. When I can, I will pay you back." Her voice was clear and firm and she didn't seem to be afraid, but Sadie knew she was. "Will you both forgive me for doing such a bad thing?"

Carl leaned back and crossed his arms over his broad chest. "I'll think about it."

Sven frowned at him, then smiled at Mary. He looked as young as Riley when he smiled. "Of course we will forgive you."

"How do we know this pretty girl is that ragged orphan boy?" asked Carl.

Mary dashed to the pile of dirty clothes and lifted up her shirt and pants. "See? Now do you believe me? Sadie cut my hair and let me wear one of her dresses. And Jewel let me wear her pretty blue ribbons." Mary touched the ribbons gently, lovingly.

Jewel pulled Mary to her side and told the bachelors Mary's story, and they interrupted from time to time with surprised comments or angry exclamations.

At last Carl reached for Mary's hand. Hesitantly she let him take it. It was lost in his big one. "Mary, I do indeed forgive you for what you did. But I don't ever want to hear of it happening again. Do you hear me?"

She nodded and pulled her hand free and rubbed it as if it burned.

Sven patted her on the head. "If you ever need help, we will help you."

"What will happen to her now?" asked Carl, looking at Jewel.

Jewel glanced at Sadie and nodded.

Sadie suddenly felt shy, but she managed to say, "She might get to live with us. I'll ask Momma and York."

"That's a lot of mouths to feed," said Sven. "Five children and another one is six."

"York can manage," said Jewel. "He's one of a kind."

Sadie felt warm inside from the kind words about York. He was her . . . her pa. She stumbled over the thought, then refused to consider it again.

13
Home Again

Sadie stepped from Jewel's barn into the bright late-morning sunlight and stopped short. Mary was still inside playing with Malachi, teaching him to shake hands. Sadie took another step, then stopped again. Near the dugout York stood talking to Jewel with Bay beside him. Sadie hadn't heard anyone ride up. She and Mary had been giggling and talking, and that had probably covered the noise. She ducked back inside. "Mary, York's here."

Mary gasped, and Malachi cocked his ears. "He is? Oh, Sadie, what if he says no?"

"He won't. I know he won't. You heard Jewel last night. He's one of a kind. He married my momma even though she had five kids, didn't he? He will be happy to have you live with us."

"Will he get mad because I'm wearing your dress?"

"No. He probably wouldn't know it was mine."

Mary peeked out the barn door. "He looks nice enough. He's a lot younger than my pa was. But he does look nice."

"He used to herd cattle for a Texas rancher. He came to Nebraska to graze 'em for the summer, and after a while of that he decided to claim his own homestead. He took his pay in cattle, and he caught a few wild horses, and that's how he got started with ranchin' for himself."

"I think I'm going to like him."

"I know he'll like you."

"Do you call him Pa?"

"No. York."

"But he is your pa."

"Kind of, I guess." Sadie rubbed a circle in the sand with her big toe. "You know my real pa died in a blizzard."

"You told me."

"York married Momma and brought us all out here last month."

"You told me. But why don't you call him Pa?"

"I feel funny about it. My pa is buried in Douglas County."

"He's dead, and now York's your pa."

Sadie finally nodded. Maybe she would call him Pa.

"I'll call him Pa if I get to live with you." Mary sighed dreamily. "He does look nice."

Sadie smiled and suddenly couldn't wait to greet him. She dashed across the yard and stopped beside Jewel. Jewel was talking, so Sadie knew no matter how excited she was she couldn't interrupt.

Finally Jewel stopped talking, and York reached out and squeezed Sadie's shoulder.

"I missed you, Sadie Rose," he said in his slow drawl.

She ducked her head, suddenly shy.

"Jewel's been tellin' me what a great help you were to her. I'm proud of you."

The praise shot right to her heart. "Thank you." Sadie finally could lift her head. She smiled into his blue eyes, and he smiled back. "Did Jewel tell you about the orphan?"

"Sure did."

"Can she live with us, York? I told her she could."

York shook his head, and Sadie's heart sank. "Sadie Rose, you shouldn't have done that. We can't take her home to your momma without asking her first. Your momma already has her hands full. She might not want another girl."

Panic rushed through Sadie. "She'd take her if you said to."

York looped his thumbs over his gunbelt. "I won't do that, Sadie Rose."

Sadie flushed hotly. She wanted to scream and kick, but she managed to say in a polite voice, "Please, York."

"Can't do it, Sadie Rose. Sorry."

Sadie stood very still as Jewel said, "I'd be pleased to have Mary stay with me tonight."

"At least that's settled," said York.

Sadie's jaw tightened.

"I'll bring her tomorrow when I come over," said Jewel. "What time are the others gettin' there?"

"Right after morning chores, I reckon." York bent down to Sadie. "Ready to go?"

She shook her head. "I . . . I have to tell . . . Mary she can't go with us."

York nodded. "Don't be long."

Sadie raced back to the barn, her head spinning. She stopped just inside the barn and for a minute couldn't see in the darkness after the bright sunlight. She didn't notice the smells of sod and manure.

Mary grabbed her arm and said in alarm, "What's wrong, Sadie? Is something wrong?"

"He won't let me . . . take you," whispered Sadie hoarsely.

Mary stumbled back and almost fell over Malachi. "I knew it! I knew he wouldn't want me! Nobody does!"

"He said we have to ask Momma first. Pa never would've asked Momma first. He'd have done what he wanted and Momma would've said okay." Sadie doubled her fists, and her face hardened. "She'd do that with York too, but he won't just take you home. He probably doesn't want any of us. Only Momma."

Mary locked and unlocked her fingers. "What will happen to me?"

"Jewel said she'd keep you with her for tonight. She said she'll take you to our place tomorrow, and then we'll know if you can stay."

"You don't think they'll let me, do you, Sadie?"

Sadie pushed her braid back. "No. No, I don't. Oh, I wish Momma had never married York! I told her not to, but she wouldn't listen to me!"

From outdoors York called, "Sadie Rose, we got to be goin'."

"What about your dress?" asked Mary in alarm.

"Wear it over tomorrow and we'll see," said Sadie. "I can't wear two dresses at the same time. If this one gets dirty, I'll wear it dirty." Anger rushed around inside her until she didn't care if she had any dresses.

"See you tomorrow, Sadie."

"Bye, Mary." Sadie wanted to say so much more, but she couldn't find the words through her anger. She walked back to York, her dragging feet stirring up dust.

Jewel patted Sadie's back. "I gave York your clothes and told him Mary is wearin' your dress. You're a good worker and a brave girl. Thanks for the help. See you tomorrow."

"Bye," whispered Sadie.

York swung into the saddle and easily lifted Sadie up behind him.

Her legs stuck almost straight out from straddling Bay's broad rump. Her skirts hiked up and showed the two colors of her skin. Instead of leaning against York's back with her arms around him, she sat stiff and gripped the back of the saddle. She smelled York's special smell, the leather of the saddle, and Bay.

"See you tomorrow, Jewel," said York.

Sadie tried to smile at Jewel, but couldn't. She saw Mary peek out of the barn again, then jump back out of sight.

York glanced back at Sadie. "Ready?"

She nodded.

York nudged Bay with his knees, and Bay walked down to the creek and along it. With a loud flutter of wings a duck flew up from the water. Sadie found Bay's rhythm and swayed with her. Wind tugged at her bonnet.

When they reached the lone cottonwood York glanced over his shoulder. "I'm sorry about Mary."

She mumbled, "It's okay." But it really wasn't.

"Maybe your momma will say yes."

"Maybe." But Momma would say only what she thought York wanted.

"Jewel told me about the bull holding you girls prisoners up in that cottonwood."

Sadie didn't say anything.

York nudged Bay, and soon Bay's thundering

hooves filled Sadie and she felt them all through her body. She ducked her head behind York to keep the wind from blowing her face off.

Several minutes later he reined to a stop near his well, and she slipped off and landed with a puff of dust.

"Sadie!" cried Helen, leaping at Sadie and hugging her tight. "You're home! You're home!"

Tanner barked and jumped against her.

Web tugged Sadie's arm. He looked glad to see her too. "Sadie, come see the deer hide. It's stretched out and dryin' in the sun at the barn."

"Oh, Sadie." Momma stood beside York and smiled at Sadie. "It feels like you've been gone for weeks instead of just a few days."

"Hello, Momma." Sadie wanted to run to Momma and hug her tight, but her anger at York held her back.

Opal and then Riley said hello, but stayed at York's other side.

"Sadie made friends with the orphan," said York with a grin.

"You did?" cried Helen and Web at the same time.

"I'd like to get my hands on him," growled Riley.

"The orphan untied Bossie the other day, and so it wasn't your fault, Helen," said Sadie. "You and Web weren't to blame." Sadie shot a look at York. "You should not have been yelled at."

"Sadie Rose York!" cried Momma. "Don't you talk that way to York."

York studied Sadie a minute and then turned to Helen and Web. "Helen and Web, I am sorry for blamin' you for something that wasn't your fault."

Sadie felt as if she'd been kicked in the stomach. Why didn't York yell at her? Why was he always so nice? She scowled. He wasn't always nice. He hadn't let Mary come home with them.

York turned back to Sadie. "Sadie Rose has quite a tale to tell about the orphan. Let's go sit in the shade of the tree and listen to her."

"Dinner's ready," said Momma.

York bent down and kissed Momma's flushed cheek, and Momma looked as if she'd been given a great gift. "We'll eat under the tree and listen to Sadie Rose."

Helen pumped Sadie's arm up and down as they walked toward the house. "What about the orphan? Oh, I can't wait to hear!"

"Is he mean and ornery like Helen said?" asked Web, bouncing along at Sadie's other side.

Sadie let them bring back her good humor, and while she sat in the shade of Momma's tree and ate dinner she told all about Mary.

When she finished the story Sadie looked at Momma. "I let her wear my other dress."

Momma smiled. She sat on a bench that York had made out of two wooden crates. "That was good of you, Sadie. You'll just have to wear your good dress tomorrow when everyone comes."

Sadie stiffened. "I can just wear this one, Momma."

"No. It's much too worn for company."

Sadie remembered Jewel asking about the others coming tomorrow and now Momma was talking about company. "Who is comin' tomorrow?"

Helen jumped around like a little flea. "Everybody! Everybody, Sadie!"

Sadie lifted her brow in question.

"Levi and his paw," said Opal smugly.

Sadie's stomach tightened.

"The bachelors from Cottonwood Creek," said Riley.

"Jewel and the orphan," said Web with a grin.

"But why?" asked Sadie, looking at her family. She could tell they knew something exciting. "What's goin' on?"

Helen jumped up and down. "Let me tell! Let me tell!"

York shook his head. "Let your momma tell."

Holding her breath, Sadie looked at Momma.

Momma smiled her pleased smile and smoothed her apron over her sturdy body. "Our friends are comin' tomorrow to help us put up a soddy big enough for all of us."

"I'll be switched," said Sadie and everyone laughed.

"You sound just like Jewel," said Riley.

"A house big enough for all of us?" Sadie looked right into York's eyes. Was it possible that Momma would say yes about Mary?

"And while everybody's here we're gonna give York his name," said Opal with pride in her voice.

Sadie could tell by the look on Opal's face that she'd found a name for York that Momma and York had liked. "What's the name?"

Opal looked very smug. "You'll all find out tomorrow. But it's a fine name. Isn't it, Momma?"

"A fine name," said Momma, squeezing York's leather-brown hand.

"We don't even know what it is," said Helen. "Not me nor Web nor Riley know."

"And you can't know either," said Opal, looking down her straight nose at Sadie.

Sadie looked at Tanner beside her and forced hateful, ugly words back. She'd wanted to say that she didn't care if York ever had a first name, that nobody cared if he did. She'd wanted to say that Opal probably had chosen a hideous name that no one would like. She'd wanted to say that and more, a whole lot more, but she knew neither Momma nor York would let her.

She rubbed Tanner's brown back and closed her ears to the excited voices of her family.

14

Forgiveness

Sadie yawned, then yawned again. "I don't know why we have to get up before the sun is even up," she grumbled.

Helen danced across the yard with her arms wide and her white braids flying in the cool wind. "Yes, you do. Today we get a house big enough for all of us. Today York gets a new name. Today company is comin'!"

"Come help me, Sadie," called Riley.

"Comin'." She ran to the back of the wagon where all five of them slept every night, the girls up at the front and the boys at the back.

As Sadie helped Riley take the cover off the wagon, she thought about Mary coming today and joy leaped inside her. She'd see Mary again. After Momma saw

Mary for herself she'd never be able to say no to her. Would she?

"Hurry, Sadie," said Riley. "Help me spread it over the pile."

The wind flapped the heavy canvas as Sadie ran to keep up with Riley's long legs. They spread the canvas over the bedding and other things they'd unloaded from the wagon. Each night they had to sleep in the wagon, but after a house was built that would be big enough for all of them they'd sleep in it. No longer would she and Riley have to take the cover off the wagon and unload the stuff just to use the wagon. They'd sleep inside on feather ticks. York had said the girls would share one bed and the boys another. They'd each have pegs for their clothes and they'd each have a space to keep their special possessions in. Sadie thought of the rag doll that she'd made and secretly kept even though she was the great age of twelve. She'd be able to keep Holly safe from prying eyes.

Suddenly Sadie twirled around the yard just like Helen had done.

Momma walked up from the barn where she'd gone to check on her hen and chicks. "Sadie, I sent Opal to get your good dress so you could it put it on."

Sadie froze. Opal would see the tear and know the terrible secret.

Just then Opal started out the door of the house, Sadie's dress in her hand. The dress caught on the door handle, and Opal tugged it free.

"I . . . I can't wear that dress, Momma," said Sadie in a strangled voice. She looked around for a way of escape.

"You have to," said Opal. "Momma said so yesterday."

Sadie had tried all yesterday afternoon to find a

way to stitch her dress without anyone seeing, but she'd never found the privacy.

"Here, Sadie." Opal held up the dress and the wind caught it, flapping it so the tear was in plain sight of Momma.

Sadie's face turned as gray as the canvas on the pile of stuff. Her legs shook, and she thought she was going to fall.

Momma ran to the dress and clutched it to her. "Opal, you tore Sadie's dress! Look at this!"

Opal looked, shaking her head in disbelief. "But I couldn't have done that. It only caught a little on the door."

"The fabric is old and tears easily," snapped Momma. "Now what will Sadie do?"

Sadie could barely believe her ears. She was safe! Momma didn't know the truth! Opal didn't know the truth! Oh, the day had never looked so beautiful!

Her round face stern, Momma shook her finger at Opal. "How could you be so careless? Sadie's only good dress!"

Opal burst into tears and covered her face with both her hands. The braids of her nutmeg-brown hair hung down to her small breasts. Wind pressed her flowered dress against her slight body. This early in the day her bare feet were still clean.

"Stop cryin', Opal, and get a needle and thread and sew up the tear."

Sadie dashed forward. "I'll do it, Momma. Don't make Opal. She feels bad already."

"You're a sweet girl, Sadie, but Opal must make amends for what she's done." Momma held the dress out to Opal and slowly, reluctantly Opal took it.

Sadie wanted to grab it out of her hands and sew it herself, but she knew Momma wouldn't let her. Pity for

Opal stirred inside her and she wanted to confess the truth, but she couldn't bring herself to do it.

"Sadie, go get breakfast on while Opal sews your dress," said Momma as she retied her bonnet under her round chin. "I'll call the others."

Sadie ran inside. She knew they were having bread and milk for breakfast, and it would only take a few minutes to slice the bread and put on the bowls and spoons.

A cake for company baked in the oven and sent out a delicious aroma. The house was already too hot for comfort because of the oven.

Opal sat beside the window to give her enough light to stitch up the dress. With teary blue eyes she looked at Sadie. "I'm sorry for tearin' your good dress."

Sadie's heart raced, and she almost dropped the stack of bowls. "Don't think nothin' of it."

"But I feel just awful!"

"Don't." Unsteadily Sadie counted out seven spoons and set them beside the bowls. She sliced thick slices of yesterday's bread and stacked it in two high piles on a plate. She filled the pitcher with milk and was ready for the others to come eat.

Momma didn't like it when all they had to eat was bread and milk, but Sadie didn't mind at all. It was one of her favorite meals, and much better than the string beans Momma would make her eat when the garden was in.

Today Momma had wanted to use the other food for company. She never wanted anyone to think that she couldn't set a good table.

After York prayed the blessing on breakfast, Sadie tore her bread into pieces and dropped them in her bowl and covered them with milk. She ate two bowls, but waited while Riley and York ate five each. Opal ate half a bowl, and Sadie knew it was because she was upset over the dress. A band tightened around Sadie's heart, and it was hard to sit still.

Finally York picked up his big black Bible and opened it to the reading for the day.

Sadie sat on the edge of Momma's and York's bed and locked her hands together in her lap. She'd been able to force back thoughts about God while she was away, but suddenly all the terrible things she'd done crashed in on her.

York read from Hebrews and when he read, "I will never leave thee, nor forsake thee," chills ran all over Sadie. York had told her God would never leave her, but she hadn't believed him. She knew she had to believe the Bible because it was God's Holy Word.

If God was always with her, then He knew everything about her.

She trembled.

Momma didn't know that she'd torn her dress.

She'd never come right out and told York she was angry with him.

She had teased Opal and had been very rude to Opal and to Levi.

God knew it all.

She bit her lip and blinked back stinging tears as York continued to read. When he said it was time to pray, he thanked God for the beautiful day and for the good friends who were helping them build the new house. He thanked God for each of them, and when he called Sadie's name she heard a special softness in his voice and she felt even worse.

Something burst inside Sadie, and while York prayed she silently told God what she'd done and that she was sorry. His Word said He'd forgive her. She knew the verse by heart: "If we confess our sins, He is faithful and just to forgive us our sins, and to cleanse us from all unrighteousness, First John 1:9." She'd learned it last year as one of her special verses at church back in Douglas County.

A heavy weight lifted off her heart, and she was able to smile when Helen asked if York was finally done.

A few minutes later, after Momma had set each one to work, Sadie stayed behind in the house.

"Momma," she said just above a whisper.

Momma frowned as she set the hot cake on the table. "Why aren't you getting the dishes done?"

"I need to talk to you." A giant tear slipped down and splashed on her hand.

Momma looked at her closely. "What is it, Sadie? Do you hurt anywhere? Do you have a tummy ache?"

Sadie swallowed hard. "Momma, Tanner tore my good dress. It was my fault. Opal didn't do it." The words rushed out before Sadie lost her nerve.

"Oh, Sadie!"

"I'm sorry that I let Opal take the blame, and I'm sorry for not tellin' you when it happened."

"Sadie, Sadie." Momma pulled Sadie close and held her.

Sadie liked the feel of Momma's soft body and the smell of her creamy skin. "I am so sorry, Momma."

"I know you are, Sadie. I forgive you. But you'll have to tell Opal what you've done." Momma held Sadie away from her. "I will have to give your punishment some thought. But then, maybe having to live with the heavy load is punishment enough. Never, never leave sin unconfessed, Sadie. It'll eat away at you and it'll kill you."

"I won't do it again, Momma."

"With God's help you won't, Sadie."

Sadie nodded. "Should I talk to Opal now, or do the dishes first?"

Momma patted Sadie's arm. "Speak with Opal first. But you must hurry. Company will be here shortly."

Sadie hugged Momma hard, then ran to find Opal in the garden where she was hoeing.

"What do you want?" asked Opal with a scowl.

For a minute Sadie thought about not saying anything to Opal, but she took a deep breath and said, "Tanner tore my dress, Opal. I'm sorry I let you take the blame."

Opal shook her head and sighed loud and long. "I should've known."

"Will you forgive me?"

"Of course. Don't I always?"

"I'm sorry for teasin' you about being an old maid that other day."

"Do you really think I'll be an old maid?"

"No."

"Then I forgive you." Opal turned back to the garden and chopped tiny little chops around the beans.

Sadie turned and ran to the barn. She didn't feel much better about Opal, but she knew she'd done what was right. Now, she had to face York. Butterflies fluttered in her stomach.

He turned from hitching up Dick and Jane. "I see by your eyes you have somethin' important to say to me, Sadie Rose."

She took a deep breath, locked her hands in front of her and said, "I was mad at you, and I thought mean things about you. I'm sorry. Will you forgive me?"

York smiled his nicest smile, and his white teeth flashed. "Yes, I will. But let me ask you somethin'."

She tensed. "What?"

"If Mary can't live with us, will you get mad all over again?"

Sadie thought about that a long time. "I'll try not to."

"If I scold you or the other kids, will you get mad?"

She hung her head.

He tipped up her chin with his finger. "Don't get mad at me for being your pa, Sadie Rose. I'm new at it, but I want to be a good pa. I love you."

She saw the love in his blue eyes, and she flung her arms around his waist just above his gunbelt and hugged him hard. "I won't get mad if you act like our pa."

He kissed the top of her head. "You'd best go change. I hear a wagon comin'."

Tanner looked toward the west and barked. Sadie flew to the house to finish her work and to change into her other dress.

15
A Name for York

Sadie touched the tiny stitches down the front of her blue gingham dress as she walked toward Levi Cass and Tanner. Opal was good with a needle, and the stitches barely showed. So far nobody had noticed the mend, and she'd been helping all day long. She'd tried to find time to speak to Levi alone, but he'd been busy bringing in sod strips Riley had plowed for the new house.

"It's too bad we couldn't finish the house today," said Levi, smiling at Sadie as she stopped beside him.

"But it'll be nice to have all of you stay the night to finish it in the morning." Sadie looked at the beautiful sod house that stood behind Momma's tree. Now the tree would shade the front door and window in the summer. York's small sod house would be used for a shed to keep cow chips in and for them to do the washing in. It seemed very elegant to have a wash house even if it was made of sod and even if they did have to use it to store winter fuel.

"Tanner's doin' good, ain't he?" Levi reached down and rubbed Tanner's neck.

"He learns fast." Sadie moved from one foot to the other. Her shoes pinched her feet, but Momma wouldn't let her go barefoot in front of company.

"Mary and Opal seem to get along just fine, don't they?" Levi frowned slightly.

Sadie turned to see Mary and Opal talking to the bachelors and laughing at something Carl White had said. Sadie couldn't wait to tell Mary that York and Momma had talked last night and had agreed to let Mary live with them.

Opal's laugh rang across the yard.

Sadie had laughed at Opal's face when she'd first met the bachelors this morning. Opal was sure she was in Heaven to have three fine young men around for the day, and now for tomorrow morning too. "Opal wants to get married when she's sixteen," said Sadie.

Levi frowned harder. "That's in two years."

"I know."

She could almost read his mind as he realized that he wouldn't be ready to get married in two years, but maybe the bachelors would.

"Are you gonna get married when you're sixteen?"

"Me?" Sadie pointed to herself, her dark eyes wide. "No! At least, I don't think so." She watched Tanner's flag of a tail wave harder as Levi scratched his ear. "Levi?"

"What?"

"I was . . . was mean to you the day you brought the deer."

"Were you?"

Sadie glanced at him, then quickly away. "It was very nice of you to bring it. And you did good gettin' it with one shot."

Levi stood taller and grinned. "Yes, I thought so. Thanks."

Before she could say more, York called everyone together for the special announcement of his name.

"It'll seem funny not to call him York," said Levi as they walked side by side to join the others under Momma's tree.

"It will be strange all right. I wonder what name Opal picked out. I hope it's not dumb." Sadie sat down with Levi beside her.

She still couldn't get used to a large sod house standing where once had been only prairie grass. The men had cut thick sod slabs and stacked them on top of each other like giant bricks. Joshua Cass called it Nebraska marble. The new house had two big rooms and three windows. It was almost too much for Sadie to imagine. One room would be the bedroom, and Momma had said that sheeting would separate it into three bedrooms. Three whole bedrooms! The other room held the cook stove and a long wooden table that York had surprised Momma with. York was building two long benches so that everyone could sit at the table at the same time. Sadie couldn't wait for them to have their first meal. She hoped it would be bread and milk.

Mary dropped down beside Sadie. "I want to talk to you later," she whispered.

Sadie nodded. She wanted to know now what Mary wanted to tell her, but Opal stood before everyone, looking poised and pretty with bright pink cheeks and sparkling blue eyes so much like Pa's.

Opal looked at the group sitting in front of her, and she smiled prettily. "As you know, York has decided

126

to take a first name. We've been studyin' on a name for him for days now. Some of you have suggested names." She looked right at Jewel, and Jewel grinned and winked. "And some of you have made jokes about it." She looked at the bachelors and they chuckled. "I made a list of men's names from the Bible." She held up the list. "We all wanted a good strong name for York."

York sat on a bench with his arm around Momma. He grinned at Opal.

"When the children of Israel were headin' into the Promised Land, Moses sent twelve spies in to see if they could take the land the way God wanted. God had told them the Promised Land was theirs. Ten of the spies came back and told everyone that there were giants in the land and that they couldn't take the land no matter what God had said. Two of the spies said they could easily take the land because God was with them even if there were giants around." Opal took a deep breath, and Sadie leaned forward eagerly. For once Opal wasn't being dumb.

"One thing I've noticed about York is that he says we can do anything with God helpin' us. He says it doesn't matter how big the problem is. He says we can take the land."

"That's right," said York.

Sadie nodded. She agreed with Opal again. It seemed strange to like Opal's idea.

Opal pushed a stray strand of nutmeg-brown hair out of her face. "The two spies were named Joshua and Caleb. We already have a Joshua. Joshua Cass. So we're givin' York the other name. Caleb. From now on York will be called Caleb York. Caleb to his friends."

The bachelors tossed their hats into the air and shouted. Jewel jumped up and slapped York hard on the back.

"Caleb it is," she said in her booming voice.

"Caleb," said Sadie softly. It sounded good to her.

Opal raised her hands and motioned for silence. "We have one more announcement. Helen's gonna give it. Helen."

Helen bounced up to the front of the crowd and looked at everyone. She twisted back and forth. The sun glowed off her white hair. "We have another name to give York. It is a very special name." She sounded as if she'd memorized a piece for the Christmas program and was reciting it. "We are going to call York Daddy."

York leaped up to Helen and scooped her high in his arms. She squealed and giggled and hugged his neck.

"That was a big surprise to me," said York in his slow drawl. "But I'm proud of the name. I'm proud of both names. An orphan like me never expected to have more than one name. If any of you forget and call me York, I'll let it go." He paused. "The first time, that is. The second time you get warned."

"The third time shot!" said Jewel with a booming laugh, and everyone joined in.

York flung his hat in the air. "Caleb York! Daddy! What more can a man want?"

"Daddy," said Sadie under her breath. Could she call York Daddy? She nodded. She could sure try.

Later she and Mary walked together out into the prairie. The sun had set, but it was still light enough to see. Lanterns were lit outside the new sod house, where the others had gathered to talk after supper.

Sadie glanced at Mary, who had her head down as she walked. "What's wrong, Mary? You've been actin' strange all day."

"I don't want you to hate me again, Sadie." Mary sounded close to tears.

"I never hated you."

"Yes, you did. When I stole your rabbit."

"I felt sorry for you."

"You did?"

Sadie stopped walking and turned to face Mary. "Why would I hate you now?"

Mary rubbed her hand on her sleeve. She still wore Sadie's dress. Momma had said she could keep it, and they would somehow work it out for Sadie.

"Just say it, Mary. You're scarin' me." Sadie shivered even though the wind was warm. Voices from the yard drifted out to them. An owl hooted. In the distance coyotes yapped.

"Sadie, me and Jewel talked it over." Mary took a deep breath. "She needs me real bad. She does, Sadie. And I need her. And Malachi. Even Annie and Ernie."

"And?" Sadie's voice broke.

"And if you aren't too upset, I want to live with Jewel."

Pain shot through Sadie's heart. "But Momma and York said you could live with us."

"I'm sorry, Sadie. Don't you see? Jewel doesn't have anyone. Only me."

Sadie thought about that a long time. Even though she ached inside, she knew Mary was right. "I won't be mad."

"You won't? Oh, Sadie!" Mary hugged her hard.

Sadie laughed. "We could be best friends, couldn't we?"

"I'd like that. I haven't had a best friend since we lived in Iowa."

"I had a best friend in Douglas County. Emma. She's a good speller. Are you a good speller?"

"Not very."

Sadie grinned. "Want to see my doll?"

"I didn't know you had a doll."

"I made her myself, and I never showed her to anyone. Her name's Holly."

"Holly and Amanda. They can be best friends too."

Sadie nodded. A rag doll and a cornhusk doll as best friends. It sounded good to her.

She looked toward the yard full of people and the new house. Standing out from all of them was York. Caleb York, her daddy. She smiled, then caught Mary's hand in hers. "Let's go look at Holly."